AN INDIVIDUAL'S INNOCENCE

The Silent Screams

Emma

Enjoy the Read

JAMES G. YEO

For all those that have been behind me all throughout this long journey. I wouldn't be here without the support.

Thank you.

Another day, another life.

FriesenPress

Suite 300 - 990 Fort St
Victoria, BC, V8V 3K2
Canada

www.friesenpress.com

Copyright © 2016 by James G. Yeo
First Edition — 2016

Photography by Ryan Wunch

ISBN
978-1-4602-9254-9 (Hardcover)
978-1-4602-9255-6 (Paperback)
978-1-4602-9256-3 (eBook)

1. FICTION, PSYCHOLOGICAL

Distributed to the trade by The Ingram Book Company

* * *

As someone with a mental illness, I understand the hard-ships that come with a diagnosis. This book is to show that it is just a diagnosis and it does not have to be the end of your life. Reach for your dreams and they will come true. Special thanks to my friends and family.

CHAPTER one

Present Time

It is the last Sunday night in March and Tammy Maxwell is watching TV when the doorbell rings. Getting out of her chair, she walks over to the window of her downtown Metro condo to see her father at the door. She runs down the steps and lets him in. "Dad, what brings you out tonight?" She hugs him as he enters.

"Does a father need a reason to come and see his little girl?" Dr. Maxwell smiles and hugs her back.

"I guess not. I'll put on a pot of coffee." Tammy lets him go and heads for the kitchen.

Taking off his shoes, Dr. Maxwell makes his way to the living room. "Where's Matt?" He takes a seat in one of the chairs.

"He's working at the hotel. There is a big banquet tonight." Tammy walks into the living room and sits in her chair. "The coffee will be ready in a few minutes."

"How are things going at work, dear?" Dr. Maxwell picks up the TV remote and turns it off.

"It's busy. And you?"

"That is why I am here. I have a patient who is being released in the morning. He says that he is going to call you and make an appointment. As well, he mentioned that you helped him before."

"Who is he?"

"You know I can't tell you that."

"What can you tell me about him then?" Tammy gets up and heads toward the kitchen to get the coffee. After pouring two cups, she puts them, along with cream, sugar, and a spoon, on a serving plate and goes back into the living room. Setting the tray down on the coffee table, she hands her father a cup.

"I have been a psychiatrist for many years and over those years I have seen many patients—but this man is the worst case I have ever had to treat. The cops and his mother brought him in."

It is the morning of January 26. In room 723, Dr. Mark Maxwell wakes up a new patient who arrived the night before. "Charles? Charles, are you awake?" he asks, shaking Charles a little.

Opening his eyes, Charles jumps out of bed and, in a startled voice, asks, "Who are you? Where am I? What's happening?"

"I'm Dr. Maxwell. You are on the seventh floor of the Metro Mental Hospital. Do you remember last night?"

"No. Why am I here?" Charles moves close to the wall with his hands behind him.

"You are here because you need help and I'm here to help you. Charles, can you tell me the last thing you remember?" Dr. Maxwell approaches Charles.

"Don't take another step," Charles says, clearly feeling like a trapped animal in a corner. He moves his hands out in front of him. "The last thing I remember is going to sleep on the twenty-fifth of December. What's the date today?"

"It is January 26. Charles, why don't you sit down on the bed?" Charles makes his way slowly to the bed and sits down. "I will talk to you a little later in the day. You should come to the activity room for some breakfast. I will show you where." Dr. Maxwell leads Charles down the hall to the activity room where other patients are eating. Charles stops at the door and Dr. Maxwell hands him a tray of food. "It's safe to go in. Nothing bad is going to happen to you here."

Charles walks in and sits down at a table.

"Tammy, he was nothing but skin and bones." Dr. Maxwell shakes his head.

"Dad, are you OK?" Tammy sips her coffee.

"The thing that makes it bad is that he didn't remember one month of his life. If his mother didn't find him, he would have died."

After breakfast ends, Charles walks back to his room and sits down on his bed, still confused about what's happening. Looking out the door of his room, he sees a glass door with an electronic lock on it. He turns to look out the window notices another bed. "What is this place?" He starts shaking his head.

"It's a hospital," a voice answers from behind Charles.

Turning around, Charles sees an older man standing in the doorway. "Who are you?"

"I'm Ryan and I'm your roommate. I heard you come in last night." He walks around Charles's bed and over to his, then sits down. "I have been here since the first."

"What are you here for?" Charles turns to face Ryan.

"I have depression and the doctor feels that I need to be here." Ryan smiles with some effort. "What are you in for?"

"I don't know but I'm sure that I'll be finding that out." Charles looks at the floor.

"Tammy, the meeting I had with him and his mother just made me realize how much help he needs."

Charles looks out to see the locked door. "We're locked down. The only difference is that there are no bars on the windows or doors."

"If you want to see it that way you can. I look at it in this way: We are all here to help one another." Ryan looks out the window.

"What do you mean by that?"

"There is a reason why we are all here and it is different for everyone. I was meant to meet you and be your roommate. The reason was to help you in your time of need." Ryan looks back at Charles.

Charles then looks out the door to see Dr. Maxwell standing in the doorway. "Charles would you like to come with me?"

"Sure," Charles gets off the bed to his feet. He follows Dr. Maxwell down the hall and into his office. He sees his mother, Janice Davis, crying in one of the chairs. "Mom, why are you here?" He takes a seat across from her.

"Mrs. Davis, your son doesn't remember what happened last night. Why don't you tell him what you told me?" Dr. Maxwell sits down.

"I went to your apartment to find you," Mrs. Davis says, sobbing. "You were hiding in your closet without any clothes on." She continued to sob. "You pushed me and the landlord out. I called the cops to get you out of your apartment and they brought you here." She brings her hands up to her eyes. "I had to save you."

"Charles, that is what happened last night."

"You should have let me die." Charles gets out of the chair and walks over to the door. "I will never talk to you again." Opening the door, he walks out.

"Mrs. Davis, we will do everything to help your son," Dr. Maxwell says, and then gets up to close the door.

"His mother was in tears but I had to ask her questions about his past. After getting the information, I had an idea of what he was going through and could be suffering from. It was either severe depression or schizophrenia. I had to then ask him some questions to be able to pinpoint what it was." He takes a sip of his coffee.

"Dad, why would he be rude with—or I should say mad at—his mother? She saved him."

"Remember, I work on a locked ward in the hospital, so I think that had a part in it and he probably didn't want to be saved."

Looking down at the floor, he continues. "I met with him again that afternoon."

Charles is sitting in the activity room playing chess against Ryan. "Who taught you how to play, Charles?" Ryan asks as he puts him into check.

"My dad, and now you are in checkmate." Charles grins.

"You tricked me." Ryan smiles and looks to the door of the activity room to see Dr. Maxwell coming in. "Here comes the doctor."

"I guess I am in checkmate now. We will have another match after supper," Charles says, as Ryan gets up from the table.

"So, you play chess, Charles," Dr. Maxwell comments, as he arrives at the table.

"You're here for me, I figure." Charles looks up at him.

"I am. I have a few questions that I would like to ask you in my office." Dr. Maxwell makes eye contact with Charles. Charles gets up from the chair and follows Dr. Maxwell to his office. As Charles takes a seat, Dr. Maxwell picks up a pen. "Now, Charles, I need you to answer these questions honestly. Do you hear voices when there is no one around?"

"I do, doesn't everyone?" Charles rolls his eyes.

"No, not everyone. Do you see things that aren't there?" He arks down the answer and looks up at Charles.

"I see spirits, if that is what you mean." Charles shakes his head and gives Dr. Maxwell a look.

Lifting his right eyebrow, Dr. Maxwell asks, "Why do you know that they are spirits?"

"Because I see my grandfather, who died when I was seventeen, all the time. I do see other spirits, as well."

"How do you tell the spirits from normal people?" Dr. Maxwell rubs his nose.

"They're in black and white. Isn't that normal?" Charles lowers his voice.

"No it's not. How long have you been seeing these spirits and hearing things?" He picks up his coffee and takes a drink.

"As long as I can remember. Why do you ask?" Charles stands up. "Are we done?"

"I just needed to know. You can go now, Charles," Dr. Maxwell sets down his coffee cup.

"It was like he thought that hearing voices and seeing things was normal for everyone," Dr. Maxwell tells his daughter, shaking his head.

"If he was dealing with that since he could remember it would be normal for him." Tammy looks at her dad's coffee cup and, seeing it empty, asks, "Dad, would you like more coffee?"

"No, that is fine." Dr. Maxwell looks out the window.

"What did you diagnose him with?"

"I diagnosed him with schizophrenia and started him on a pill treatment. Before I told him, I found him playing chess again by himself."

It was the morning of the twenty-seventh, and Charles was playing chess with Ryan. "So Ryan, when do you get to leave?" Charles moves his queen, putting Ryan into check.

"When the doctor feels that I am ready to go home." Ryan moves his knight taking the queen. "Here comes the doc."

Dr. Maxwell walks over to the table. "Playing chess again, I see." He smiles.

"I guess. What else do you think I should do? Should I sit here alone and go crazy?" Charles makes another move, this one placing Ryan into checkmate.

"Charles, nice move. I'm out of here, we will play another game after lunch." Ryan gets up from the table and walks out of the activity room.

"You must be a good player because you beat black yesterday, too. Do you have a moment?" Dr. Maxwell motions for Charles to get up.

"Moments are all I have now, so I guess." Getting up from the table, Charles then followed Dr. Maxwell to his office. He walks in the door of the office he sees his mother and his Aunt Brenda. "What are they doing here?"

"They're here because you will need all the support you can get today. Charles, there is no easy way to tell you this, but you have schizophrenia. I'm starting you on a pill treatment tonight." Dr. Maxwell makes eye contact with Charles. "You will be in the hospital for some time as we need to get the right dosage for the medication."

"No. I would rather live on the streets before being in lockdown on this floor," Charles says, shaking his head.

"You do have a choice. You can volunteer to be here or I will commit you. If you volunteer, you will get privileges to leave the floor and the hospital with your aunt and other family members. On the other hand, if I commit you, you will not get the freedom until I feel that you're no longer a flight risk. So what will it be?" Dr. Maxwell leans toward Charles.

"Fine, I'll stay, but I want a binder full of paper, pens, and some art supplies so I can draw and write." Charles throws his head back.

"Mrs. Davis, can you get him those things for him and clothes?" Dr. Maxwell relaxes back in his chair.

"Brenda and I can do that." Mrs. Davis looks over at Charles. "We're just trying to help you, son. That's all."

"Charles is there anything else you would like?" Brenda gets Charles's attention.

"No, just what I said. That should do me for a few months." Charles covers his eyes. "Can I go, doctor?"

"You can go, Charles," Dr. Maxwell says, as Charles uncovers his eyes and gets up from the chair.

"I didn't know how he was going to take it. After he left the office, I talked to his mother and aunt and let them know that he would be in good hands." Dr. Maxwell starts rocking back and forth in the chair.

"Dad, what is wrong?" Tammy asks, with concern in her voice.

"All the tests we did on him came back normal. I think I made a mistake in diagnosing him. He might have been having a mental breakdown." Dr. Maxwell brings his hands over his eyes.

"If he was seeing things and hearing voices, you didn't make a mistake, Dad."

"I know that those are the signs of it, but there is little we truly know about the human mind. The little we do know is only to the tip of the iceberg. Who am I to say what is normal and what isn't?" Dr. Maxwell stops rocking.

"Dad, we know more than that. You have been working in mental health for years, so you know what is normal."

"How do we not know if it is the evolution of the human mind and we are calling it an illness?" Dr. Maxwell shakes his head. "That night, I started him on the pill treatment."

Charles is sitting in the activity room playing cards with Ryan. "Charles, are you spiritual?" Ryan looks at Charles.

"I am. I have gone through a lot so I feel that this place is just another test. Why do you ask?" Charles grins.

"The reason is because your eyes tell a different story. Have you accepted your past and forgiven those who have hurt you?" Ryan makes eye contact.

"Are you passing judgment on me? I just met you yesterday. Who are you to me? You are in here, as well," Charles says, raising his voice.

"Charles, I am here by choice and raising your voice only means that there are things that you are hiding from. I'm not judging you. If you don't make peace with your past, it will kill you. Start by writing it out so that way it is in front of you and then the rest will fall into place like it should." Ryan gets up from the table.

"Who are you? Buddha?"

"That is one of the names I go by." Ryan walks away from the table.

Charles looked down the hall as Ryan walks back to the room. He glances at the clock and sees that it is ten. Getting up from the table, he walks out of the activity room. As he passes the nurse's station, he's stopped by one of the nurses, "Charles, time for your pills."

"I'm not taking those," Charles remarks, with a look to kill on his face.

"There are two ways we can do this. Either you take the pills willingly or we do it by force. How would you like to do it?" The nurse looks him square in the eyes.

He puts out his hand. "Fine, I'll take the pills."

"Here is some water to take with them."

"Are these going to make me normal?" Charles asks, swallowing them. "Good night, nurse." He walks into his room. "Ryan, I have some questions for you." He opens the curtain that divides the room to see no one. He then looks to see that the bathroom door is open. Charles walks out to the nurse's desk. "Where is Ryan?"

"Who?" The nurse looks up from a file.

"Ryan. He walked past here a couple of minutes before me." Charles taps his fingernails on the desk.

"There is no Ryan on this floor," the nurse says, making eye contact with Charles.

"My roommate, Ryan," Charles says, getting annoyed.

"You don't have a roommate, Charles." The nurse turns back to the file.

"The nurse told me that he stood at the desk for a few minutes before he went back to his room. So that is when he knew he was seeing them in colour, as well. The next day, I sat down with him after breakfast."

Charles sits at the back table by himself in the activity room. "It's the twenty-eighth today, Charles," Dr. Maxwell says, sitting at the table across from him.

"What does it matter? I'm in here with no place to go. I only hope that this is the worst part of my life." Charles looks out the window. "You must have heard what happened last night."

"I did, but I'm not here to talk about that. I'm here to find out if you are OK," Dr. Maxwell says, looking down at the table and seeing that the chessboard is set up. "Do you want to play?"

"Maybe another time, and I am fine or whatever 'fine' may be."

"You know Charles, there are people around you that love you and want to help. I, myself, know that you can live a normal life and reach your goals. This diagnosis is not the end of your life; there are many people who have done great things who suffer from schizophrenia."

"I think I will go and play that piano in the other room, that might lift my spirits." Charles gets up out of the chair and walks to the room where the piano is.

Dr. Maxwell follows. "Charles, I believe that you are meant to be here and you are wanted."

"You know, doc, you don't have to explain why I am here. I am sick. So do your job." Charles sits down at the piano.

"Charles, do you believe in God?"

"Dr. Maxwell, I can see things that you can't. I know what I see and I know God." Then with a snort, he continues, "If there was a God, I wouldn't be in here. Now go and leave me in peace." He starts playing the piano.

"That sounds good. I will talk to you later."

"He changed that day. I don't know if he was touched by God or if he was just realizing that he was going to be in the hospital for a while." Dr. Maxwell turns to Tammy.

"Dad, I think that everyone is touched by God in some way when they're in the hospital, and more so in the mental wards." Tammy finishes her coffee and gets up for more.

"I don't know. I think that the people with mental illness are the true image of God, in a way," says Dr. Maxwell, also standing. "I think I will have another cup."

"Dad, did this guy play you every day, or did he make you see the light?" Tammy hands her dad a cup of coffee and they walk back to the living room.

"I guess he made me see the light. I haven't been to church in many years, and that Sunday I went. Anyway, his mother and aunt showed up with the things he wanted and some clothes."

Charles is sitting in his room quietly waiting for the time to go by when his mother walks through the door. "Here are the things you wanted, Charles." She places a couple of bags on his bed. "We also got you some clothes and shoes."

"Thanks," he says in a low voice, looking at the bags.

"Are you OK, Charles?" His mother sits down on the bed beside him.

"I'm fine. Just go. Go home, mom. I'll be here for some time, and when the doctor feels that I'm ready to be released, I'll come home then," Charles says, bringing his hand up to his eyes and starting to cry. His Aunt Brenda walks into the room.

"Charles, your mother is going to be here for the next four days and your grandparents are coming to see you tomorrow." Brenda sits down on the other side of him.

"Aunt Brenda, I don't need the family to see me like this." Charles shakes his head back and forth as the tears run down his face.

"The reason why they want to see you is because they love you." His mother puts her arm around him.

"Why don't you come back tomorrow, when the family is here. I don't feel like having people around me today." Charles closes his eyes.

"We will see you tomorrow afternoon then." His mother gets up and leaves the room.

"Charles, I will see you later. Take care," Brenda gets up and leaves, as well.

"Tammy, after they dropped his things off, he took the binder and a pen and sat down in the activity room. He started to write."

Charles is sitting at the back table on the right side of the activity room looking outside. He opens up his binder and begins to write. "This is the journal of Charles Logan Davis. In these pages, I'll reflect on my life." He turns the page and puts a number one in the top right-hand corner. "Today is January 28," he writes, and leans back in the chair and looks outside. *What do I write?* he thinks. Looking back down to the table, he writes, "I was brought to this hospital for help. Now I will start to help myself. I was a baby once, innocent, and then I grew up. I have had my ups and downs through my life like everyone else. I'm now locked down in this mental ward with no way out except passes which I have not received yet. I was diagnosed with schizophrenia, and I'm now on pills. Last night, I thought I had a roommate but I didn't. Who was Ryan? Was he sent to me by God?" Charles looks up to see a young black girl sitting down across from him at the table.

"What are you doing?" She makes eye contact with him.

"I'm writing. What are you doing?" Charles asks, in his monotone voice.

"I'm Liz. Who are you?"

"I'm Charles. I don't mean to be rude, but you can go. I'd like to be alone." Charles puts his hands behind his head, shaking it.

"Charles, I hope that you don't have hate in your heart." Liz gets up and walks out of the activity room.

Looking down at the table, he picks up his pen and starts to write again, "Ryan said that I needed to make peace with my past and forgive those who hurt me. Maybe that is the real reason why I'm in here: to get over my past. I must say that I haven't been an angel in my life, and I ask God for forgiveness. I have done things that I'm not proud of. In Cunnings, I was trafficking drugs and in those four years, I had to kill. Whoever reads this is going to ask why I did that ,so I will answer that question. I was mad at the world because of what happened to me in Prussia. I didn't care who I hurt. All I wanted to do was die and I thought and wished every night in those four years that I would piss someone off and they would kill me. It never happened, luckily.

"I remember the first person I killed. He was a low-life and didn't understand what he was doing. He crossed my boss, and me and two other guys that ran with me were sent to kill him. We picked him up from where he worked, got him high and took him to the centre of the old train trestle which separates the north and south of the city. It's about a hundred-story drop into the river below. Logan and Jay, the other two with me, held him on each side. I pulled out my gun and shot him between the eyes. Then they let him go and he fell off the trestle into the river below." Charles closes his eyes and sets the pen down. Shaking his head, he opens his eyes and looks out the window.

"Is this seat taken?" a female voice asks.

Charles turns his head and sees a young lady standing beside the table. "No. You can sit down if you want to."

"I'm Abby. What is your name?" Abby sits down at the table.

"Charles," Charles smiles and looks her in the eyes.

"Are you writing a book?" Abby points to the binder.

"No, I'm just doing a journal to reflect on my past. How long have you been here for?" Charles breaks eye contact.

"I came in yesterday. I suffer from deep depression. What are you suffering from?"

"The doctor said schizophrenia. I was diagnosed yesterday with it. So, I will be here for some time, I feel."

"Charles, where are you from?" Abby picks up the deck of cards from the table and begins to shuffle them.

"I'm from Hillsdale, a few hours north of here. Where are you from?" Charles picks his pen back up and taps it on the paper.

"I'm from here. I'll talk to you later and maybe we could play crib." Abby gets up from the table.

"You don't have to leave if you don't want to." Charles sets his pen back down.

"That's OK. I think that I will go and do some writing of my own," Abby says, and walks away.

Charles looks down at what he has written and picks up his pen. He begins to write again. "For those of you who think I am a monster for doing what I did in Cunnings, I don't want you to change your mind or feel sorry for me. I only ask God for forgiveness for what I have done because I have done wrong and it's Him who I'll be answering to when I die." Charles puts his pen into the pocket on the inside of the binder and closes it.

"Tammy, in those two months he made me question God. Why would a person have to go through what he had to go through? He was never diagnosed when he was younger. If he was, he would have been placed on the right drugs and he would never have come through the doors of the hospital." Dr. Maxwell sits back down in the living room.

"Everything happens for a reason, Dad. I have learned that over the last three years from my clients. With that knowledge, I have changed how I counsel my patients and it has made me better at what I do." Tammy sits down with her coffee. "How did he make you question God?"

"I don't know, but he did. He once asked me if I believed in God. That happened in his third week on the floor. He told me that we walked blind through life and that our lives are written for us. That is the reason why we are blind."

"You know, Dad, I had a client like that about three years ago. He was full of himself, but I could see something in him. He made me question more than God. He made me question myself and all the decisions that I had made in my life." Tammy looks up at the clock and sees that it is eight.

"The day his grandparents were coming I pulled him into my office."

"Charles, how are you feeling today?" Dr. Maxwell opens Charles's file.

"I'm fine. These pills are already messing me up." Charles grins.

"It will take a week or so until you get use to them. So your grandparents are coming to see you today. Are you looking forward to seeing them?" Dr. Maxwell leans back in his chair.

"Why are you asking me?"

"I'm only wondering if you are looking forward to seeing them."

"Well, let me ask you a question. If you were in my shoes would you be looking forward to see them?" Charles asks harshly.

"I would be happy that they were on their way to see me."

"You got your answer—let's leave it like that." Charles gets up out of the chair. "Are you a family man, doc?"

"I am." Dr. Maxwell turns his head a little to the right, unsure of where this is going.

"How would you feel if one of your family members was in a place like this?" Charles walks up to the desk.

"I would feel helpless."

Charles picks up a picture that was on the desk, "Is her name Tammy?"

"Yes, that's my daughter. How do you know her name?" Dr. Maxwell makes eye contact with Charles.

"She was my therapist a few years back. Anyway, are we done with the questions?" Charles walks backward to the door of the office. Dr. Maxwell nods yes.

"When he said your name, I knew that he was getting ready to play a game with me. I saw it and then got ready for it, but it never happened." Dr. Maxwell puts his coffee down. "To be honest, when he said your name, I feared for you."

"Dad, I'm safe and I know that no harm will come to me. If he is a former patient of mine, he will probably call and make an appointment to see me."

"After his grandparents left, he played the piano for hours. A couple of days later, other family members came to the hospital. I watched him closely, and over the two months, he changed. I asked him if he found God and he told me that he had found peace." Dr. Maxwell takes a breath.

"That's good if he found peace."

"So, Tammy, if you get a call from him in the next couple of days, be ready." Dr. Maxwell looks at the clock. "I must get home because your mother is probably worried about me." He walks to the door and puts on his shoes.

"Dad, thanks for coming over and letting me know. Take care." Tammy walks over to him and gives him a hug.

"Take care." Dr. Maxwell opens the door of the condo and leaves.

Tammy returns to the living room and starts to wonder who it could be.

CHAPTER two

The morning came fast and Matt had already left for work. After getting ready, Tammy makes herself a breakfast shake and leaves, too. As she walks toward her office, she stops to get a newspaper from The News on the corner of Morris and South Streets.

"Just the paper today, Tammy?" the cashier asks as he opens the till.

"Yeah, just this today, Rob." Tammy gives him the money.

"The jackpot is $18 million on Wednesday. Could I interest you in a ticket?"

"Maybe I'll get one." Tammy hands him a five.

"Remember me if you win."

"I will. Have a good day, Rob," Tammy says with a smile as she walks out. She walks up Morris to Park Street and turns right toward the Public Gardens. As she reaches the Gardens, she crosses the street to the office building. Opening the door of the office building, she walks in past Café de Rock on the right side of the lobby. "Good morning Nick," Tammy says, as she passes the security desk.

"Good morning, Tammy," Nick says, leaning back in his chair.

Tammy continues to the elevators, pushes the button and waits for it to come. The door opens and she walks in and pushes for the sixth floor. When the doors open, she walks out and heads to her office. Carolin, Tammy's friend and assistant, is busy with a phone call. Tammy walks by and sits down in her office. She looks at the files on her desk for a moment to find out who has appointments for the day. Turning in her chair, she looks out of her window to see the Gardens. A few minutes pass, and Carolin walks into the office.

"How are you today, Tammy?" Carolin takes a seat in one of the two leather chairs in front of Tammy's desk.

"It's Monday, and I'm good." Tammy turns the chair to face Carolin and continues. "And how are you today?"

"I can't complain, and if I did no one would listen anyway." She laughs and puts a piece of gum into her mouth. "How was your weekend?"

"My weekend was fine, I guess, other than Matt worked the whole time. My dad did come over for coffee last night. He said that he was releasing one of his patients today and the guy is a former client of ours. Dad said that we should be ready for a call from him."

"He didn't mention the name of the guy so we would know who we could be getting a call from, did he?"

"No, he didn't. You know the rules of the health field, so be ready for the call."

"I'm ready for anything that gets thrown at me, so I hope he calls today. Tammy, after work today, do you want to go for a coffee at Mark's?" Carolin relaxes into the chair.

"We could do that and then I'll tell you who I think it could be." She looks at the clock and says, "it's five to nine—time to help some people."

Carolin smiles. "I guess it's that time." She gets up from the chair and walks out into the waiting room to her desk.

When the last of Tammy's patients has left the office, Carolin says, "It's five, and are you ready to go?"

"I'm ready. Just needed a second to come back to earth. I had a sudden feeling of sorrow. I don't know where it came from." She gets out of her chair.

"Who knows? Maybe hearing people telling you their life stories to you for five days a week might have brought it on."

"It's not that. It's almost like I feel sorry for this person who may call. You know what I mean?" They make their way to the office door.

"I think so." Carolin opens the door to the hallway and shuts off the lights.

"Well, let's go to Mark's." Tammy closes the door and locks it.

Tammy and Carolin walk out of the building, and turn left to walk to the lights. At the lights, they turn left again and walk down Spring Street toward the waterfront where Mark's is located, a ten-minute walk down the street. Getting their coffees, they head to the patio and sit down at a table for two. They both take a sip of their coffees.

"For a small port city, Metro has a lot of naval traffic." Carolin smiles as a cargo ship passes by.

"It does, I could only guess what rent would be for an office down here. Carolin, how long have we been friends?"

"I think since grade five or six." Carolin takes a sip of her coffee.

"We went to university together to become counsellors and we have been working together since we opened the office. We have a good history together." Looking out over the harbour, she takes a sip of her coffee.

"We have had our ups and downs over the years, but we still remained friends. As well, I got Matt into your life. What are you getting at?"

"I think that Matt and I are falling apart. He works all the time and when he is not at work, he is thinking about it. You know that he is a sous chef now, and him being always at work is killing me inside. He is never at home. I'm normally asleep when he gets home and sometimes he is gone before I leave for work." She tries to hold back the tears that are welling up.

"What do you two do on his days off?" Carolin places her hand on Tammy's hands.

"Days off, if he gets them, are Mondays and Tuesdays, but they are so short-staffed he is working today. When we are together, we fight. I don't think I can do it anymore." A tear falls from her eye.

"Tammy, maybe he is working this hard to make it easier for the two of you in the future."

"I remember something that one of our patients said about cooking. He said that relationships don't last. Matt brings his work home with him and I can see the stress in his eyes. I have told him time after time to quit that job and look for something else, or go to school. I'm sorry Carolin, I shouldn't be venting on you."

"It's OK. That's what friends are for. Let's change topics before you really start to cry. Who do you think this person who might call is?"

"I think that it's going to be Charles Davis. The more that Dad talked last night about the patient, the more it sounded like him." Looking through the windows into the coffee shop, she thinks she sees Charles.

"Him, after he left the office for the last time three years ago, you said that you didn't think he would be back. Not to mention all the problems you had with him from day one. What did you see in him to keep letting him come back?"

"I saw a lost man who was alone in the world. It took me some time to break him down and at times he was a jerk to me. I saw through it and saw him for who he was and what he could become with the right guidance." Turning her head back, Tammy makes eye contact with Carolin.

"So what you are telling me is that this jerk might be the one calling us. Why do you think it is him? Really."

"I had a feeling that he would fall and end up in the hospital. You must fall down before you realize that the old ways don't work and you need someone to pick you up and show you the way. That's why I think it's him."

<hr>

Session One

It's the first Monday of April, three years earlier. Tammy and Carolin are opening the doors on their new careers by starting a practice as therapists.

"Tammy, are you ready to help people?" Carolin asks, as they both walk through the doors of their new office on the sixth floor overlooking the Public Gardens.

"I am. I still can't believe this day has come." Tammy smiles, knowing that one of her dreams has come true.

"How does it feel?"

"There are no words to describe how I feel. All I know is that it feels like a heavy weight has been taken of my shoulders." Tammy sits down in one of the chairs.

"Well, we only have three clients today: two in the morning and one after lunch at two." Carolin opens the appointment book.

"Let's get ready then." Tammy gets up and walks into her office. She sits down in her chair and looks out of her window to see the Public Gardens.

The first two appointments go well and Tammy and Carolin go for lunch at the restaurant on the main floor. After a short conversation about how the morning went they return to the office to wait for the last patient. At ten to two, the door of the office opens and a man walks in dressed in black army boots, ripped jeans, a white tee-shirt. He wears blue-tinted glasses on his well-groomed face, and his hair is done in a Caesar cut. At six foot and with perfect physique, he makes his way to one of the chairs in the waiting room.

"Are you Charles Davis?" Carolin asks him as she looks up from her computer.

"That is my name."

"Ms. Maxwell is waiting, so you can go in." Carolin returns to her work on the computer.

Charles walks into Tammy's office. "May I take a seat?"

"You may, Charles," Tammy nods and smiles. Charles takes a seat in one of the two leather chairs in front of her desk. "How are you today?"

"I'm fine. You have a nice view of the Public Gardens from up here," Charles says ,with a monotone voice.

"Thank you. Do you mind if we record these sessions?" Tammy pulls out a recorder.

"I don't mind." Charles looks out the window on his left.

"Well Charles, let's get started. Tell me, why you are here?" Tammy pushes record.

"The reason I'm here is because my boss thinks that I need help. Why are you here?" He shakes his head back and forth.

"I'm here to help people," Tammy says.

Cutting Tammy off ,he says, "Don't give me that crap. You're here because of your father. Dr. Mark Maxwell is your father, right?" Charles looks at the picture of her father on the wall.

"He is. Why are you being hostile?"

"I'm just messing with you, but I do know who your father is."

"Charles, why does your boss think you need the help?"

"I don't know myself. All I know is that he said if I don't get any help I'd lose my job. So where do you want to start?" He cracks his knuckles as he waits for Tammy to answer.

"Are you from Metro?" Tammy picks up a pen.

"No I'm not. I moved down here on May 23, last year. That was the day I left my parents' place in Sova." He leans to his left and rests his chin on his hand.

"You are from Sova then."

"Wrong. You shouldn't try to guess; just ask the right question and you will always get the answer you are looking for," Charles snorts.

"Well then, where are you from?" Tammy taps her pen on the desk.

"Where was I born or the last place? Wait a minute, I already told you the last place I lived," he says with a laugh that would even scare the meanest person. He waits for her to respond.

"Are you done yet?" Tammy rolls her eyes.

"You know, we are going to enjoy this time that we will be spending together. You are just going to have to learn to ask the right questions. That will come in time." Smiling at her, he continues. "I was born in Capotell, a three-hour drive north of here, on April nineteenth, twenty-four years ago. That would make me twenty-three this year and it happens to be on a Monday. My first home was in Hillsdale, which is an hour southwest of Capotell. I lived there until I was seven and then we moved."

"Where did you move to?" She writes a note.

"Prussia, but we will talk about that later." Looking at the art on the wall behind Tammy, he smiles.

"Bad memories," Tammy is able to say before Charles cuts her off again.

"I said we will talk about it later."

"OK, we will talk about it another day. Do you have brothers or sisters?" she inquires in an effort to break the ice with him.

"I do. My brother is six years older and works with computers. My sister is four years older and is a teacher. I'm the baby." Charles breaks eye contact and looks out the window.

"Do they live down here?"

"No, they don't. My brother lives in Toon and my sister lives in Jasmine." Rolling his eyes, he slips into a different world.

"Charles, tell me: What is life like down here compared to in Sova?" Seeing that he's somewhere else, she closes her eyes and shakes her head.

"You're new at this aren't you? Simply put, you don't have to fight for a job out there. It's a different way of life and it's hard to explain. It's like comparing apples to oranges."

"Charles, just tell me about your life. If we are going to be meeting with each other every week, I should get to know who you are." She puts down her pen in frustration.

"If that's the case, your file on me is going to be thick. Let's get started for real now. I think we will go to two years before I was born. My mother had her tubes cut, burnt and tied. My parents didn't want another child. I'm what is known as a miracle child because I'm the only child born after that type of operation. Makes you think, doesn't it?" He rubs his nose, knowing the game is just beginning.

"How do you know that?" Tammy asks, confused with what he has said.

"I think that it was an uncle or grandparents who told me when I was six. When I was older, I asked if it was true, and they said that it was. A few years later when I was living in Cunnings, I did some looking into it, and that was when I found out that I was the only one." Looking into Tammy's eyes, he continues. "You don't believe me."

"It's not that..." Tammy says, before Charles cuts her off once again.

"No, that's what it is. You don't believe me. Call Dr. Bill Roberts at the Capotell General Hospital and he will tell you the same thing. All you have to do is mention my full name. Trust me."

"I believe you. I guess you were meant to be. How do you feel about that?" She tries not to laugh.

"How would you feel if you found out that you were a child who wasn't wanted?" he asks and clears his throat. "Don't answer. I wake every morning wondering if I was wanted."

"When your parents told you the truth, it must have torn you apart." She leans back into her chair, thinking she has put him into check.

"It did, and turned my world upside down." He closes his eyes.

"Let's change topics then. What all places have you lived up until now?" She picks her pen back up, ready if he is.

"You call that changing topics?" Laughing and shaking his head, he continues. "I lived in Hillsdale until I was seven, then we moved 4,000 kilometres west of Hillsdale to Prussia. We lived there until I finished grade eleven and then moved to Sova, which is two hours north of Prussia. I finished school in Sova and, that summer, moved to Cunnings, a three-hour drive northwest of Sova. I spent four years there and moved back to Sova three months after my twenty-second birthday. I lived at home for almost a year before moving down here."

"It sounds like you moved around a lot." Tammy takes a sip of her water and realizes she is starting to feel sorry for him.

"Up until now, I have changed addresses twelve times. Try living your life like that." He leans back and puts his feet up on the desk.

"Get your feet down," she says, pushing them off of the desk. "Charles, how do you feel about moving around so much?"

"I knew this was going to be a waste of time," he continues, shaking his head. "With all the education that you had to go through to do your job, you are following the book. You are using the same old questions that every other psychologist uses. Do they give all the new and want-to-be psychologists the same book, *Psychology for Morons*? Really, do the teachers at the school teach you to not think about the questions that you are going to ask?"

"I'm only asking the questions that any other therapist would ask and why are you questioning the methods I was taught in school?" Tammy asks in a defensive tone.

"Are you like every other therapist or are you different? The reason I'm questioning your methods is because they don't work. Everyone is different; that is why they don't work."

"You came to me for help and I only can help you if you want it." She drops her pen as she can see he has no intention to play fair.

"Make no mistake, I was sent here and I have to keep coming here so I can keep my job," he says, raising his monotone voice.

"It was just a simple question," Tammy says, raising her own voice.

"How do you think I would feel about moving around as much as I did?" Charles stands up and points at her.

"I don't know. That's why I asked you. Maybe you don't know what you feel because no one has ever asked you." Tammy slams her hand on the desk.

"I think you have asked enough questions for this session. I'll see you next Monday at two." Getting up, Charles leaves the office.

"Tammy, Tammy, you OK?" Carolin waves her hand in front of Tammy's eyes.

"Yeah, I'm fine. What's wrong?" Tammy grabs Carolin's hand.

"You were in the middle of a sentence and then you drifted off into space."

"I was just remembering that first session we had with Charles," Tammy laughs. "If I had been any other therapist, it would have been the last one. I felt that I could help him, and that's why I didn't pull the plug on him."

"If it's him that is going to be calling, do you think he has changed?" Carolin finishes her coffee.

"I hope he did, but we won't know until he makes that call." Tammy gets up from the table. "Well, I guess it's time to head home."

"Yeah." Carolin gets up, too. They walk out the doors of Mark's. "I'll see you in the morning, Tammy."

"Have a good night, Carolin," Tammy says, and starts up the hill to her condo. She opens the door, checks the mail, and walks into the house. "Bill, bill, letter," she mutters. After taking her shoes off, she goes into the kitchen, sets the mail on the table, and makes herself something to eat. After, she goes into the living room and sits down in her chair. Leaning back she closes her eyes....

Two o'clock comes and Charles walks into Tammy's office and closes the door. "Good afternoon, Ms. Maxwell. May I take a seat?" Charles points to one of the chairs.

"You may, Charles." Tammy opens up his file. "How are you today?"

"I'm well. It's a beautiful day out today." He sits down in the same chair as the last time. "I wonder how a person like you gets an office like this. Art on the walls, all your books, a globe, these leather chairs, that big desk, and a nice view of the Public Gardens. Not to mention a piece of paper from Atlantis University, which is framed with your name on it, on the wall behind you. I hope that all of this didn't put a dent in your dad's pocket book."

"Do you like my office, Charles?"

"I guess it's nice if you want to give the impression that you are better than your patients. This works. Oh, all those books you have there in your bookshelf, including the schoolbooks, I've read, but the difference is that the cost was all of a library card. That was free," he laughs.

"May we begin, Charles?" Tammy replies. She is becoming annoyed with him.

"If I have that tone right, you are getting upset. Sorry. I didn't want to rain on your parade, but it's so easy." Smiling at her, he continues. "Let's begin. Where would you like to start?"

"Last week, we talked some about your mother having her tubes tied before she had you. How often do you think about that?" She looks down her nose at Charles.

"Were you not listening when I told you? You even have that stupid machine recording our conversations. So, to remind you, I think about it all the time. I wonder if I was wanted, and the answer I always find is no. The reason I say this is because if they had wanted me, they wouldn't have had the operation."

"Do you feel that your life has a special purpose?"

"Doesn't everyone have a reason to be here? The reasoning for my life is no different than theirs. If you mean did God put me here for a reason, I would say yes to that. I haven't found out why yet, that's all." Charles turns to the window.

"Does it bother you not knowing why you are here?"

"Not really, because when I'm ready to know, I'll know. Just a little piece of information for you: when I get mad at my parents, I bring up the fact that they had the operation and I always say that I wished that it would have worked." He turns back to face Tammy and makes eye contact with her.

"Why do you say that?" Tammy looks away.

"It shuts them up and makes them listen to me. Go figure—I play dirty."

"I think we will change topics now that I got everything I needed out of that one. Last week, I asked you how you felt about moving so much. Are you ready to answer the question now?" She picks up a pen and makes a note in his file.

"You really didn't learn anything in school, did you? What did I tell you last week? You are going to learn more from me than what you learned in school? You want to know how I feel? I'm numb to it, Ms. Maxwell. I've moved around so much that I'm unable to find a place where I can call home. The longest I've stayed in one area is ten years; the only downfall is that we moved five times in that community. I haven't put down any roots because I never know where I'm going to be."

"I see. Tell me, Charles, what does your father do for a living?" Tammy makes another note.

"He is the administrator of the hospital in Sova."

"Has he always worked in health care?"

"He has. That's one of the main reasons we left Hillsdale. He got a job in Prussia as the director of operations at the nursing home."

"Charles, is that when the moving began?" She jots down a few more notes.

"That is when it started on a big scale. As I said, we moved several times in that town. I don't blame my parents for what happened in Prussia because they were only trying to make a better life for us kids." Looking down at his feet, he closes his eyes.

"What does your mother do?"

"Other than worry about me, she works in one of the banks in Sova. When we lived in Prussia, she worked in the drugstore and I can't remember where she worked when we lived in Hillsdale. I'm surprised you're not asking me about my upbringing."

"That will come. I feel we need to work with you more before we touch on that. Charles, do you remember much about when you lived in Hillsdale?"

"I do. It was the best seven years of my life. The village is about a thousand people strong. There are farms on the south side of the village and, to the north, a small mountain. As well, there are two rivers running through, one flowing north to south, which empties into the other that goes east to west. The school is near the east-west river on the north bank of the river. We lived on the mountain until I was six and then we moved into a nicer house that was beside the east-west river. I still remember walking into the old schoolhouse. I was in kindergarten and it was during the winter. The grade fours were taking us skating at the outdoor rink. I couldn't skate then and I still can't." He looks out the window. "Everything was great I had friends and I didn't have a care other than being happy. Then one day during grade two, Dad tells us that we are moving to Prussia. Dad left that March; we followed when school was finished. We took the bus with Mom."

"Charles, was your dad home much when you lived in Hillsdale?"

"I can't remember. All I knew was that he worked at the hospital as an orderly and it was shift work."

"I see. Charles, when your parents were at work, who watched you?"

"For the few hours after school when my parents were at work, my brother and sister watched me." He brings his hands together.

"Here, Ms. Maxwell, I will tell you how these sessions are going to work. First, save the questions from the book because I told you that they don't work. Secondly, what I'll do is talk about my past and other subjects. When a question comes to you, think about it and then ask yourself the question to see if it is a stupid one. This way, you will stop asking stupid questions. Understand?"

"I do. I am only trying to understand you."

"Understand me? It's easy. Don't ask stupid questions. You have to open your ears and mind and shut your mouth if you are going to ask something stupid. With this knowledge, you will be able to listen to your clients and help them more. My boss told me to get help but he didn't say with whom. Your Dad talks to other people in the health-care field and my dad is one of them. Dad knew that you were opening this practice and that is why I chose you. The other reason is because I know that I can help you become a better counsellor. Think outside the box and you will become better than the best today. Do you comprehend?" He cracks his knuckles.

"Where do you want to start then?" She lets out a sigh.

"I guess I will start when we moved to Prussia. Like I said, we took the bus, which was a good four-day trip to Speed, which is an hour-and-a-half southeast of Prussia. My dad was at the bus station waiting for us. As we drove to Prussia, I looked out the window to see the landscape of the prairie. When you go from trees to seeing grain fields, the change is shocking. When we finally got to Prussia, I wanted to know where the forest and rivers were. The closest river was a ten-minute drive north of town and the forest was much further. Anyway, Prussia is a town of about a thousand souls and most of the people are farmers."

"Sounds like a nice little farm town."

"Yes, it is a little farming town, but not nice. For the ten years that I lived there, I learned what the meaning of the word hate was." Leaning back into the chair, he continues. "I'll get into that in another session because the memories to this day still bother me."

"The memories are that bad?"

"They are and that is one of the reasons why I see things in a different way."

"Charles, what do you mean that you see things differently?"

"Almost everyone sees in black and white and thinks inside the box. I see in colour and think outside the box."

"Doesn't everyone see in colour?"

"You're missing the point that I'm trying to make. You of all people should understand because it's written in your textbooks. I was told by one of the psychologists that I saw in Cunnings to describe it that way to people so they would understand. In your case, you didn't."

"I did understand what you were saying. I just never heard it that way before. What you are saying is that you are different. Am I right?"

"You're close. Feel free to ask a question, but make sure you think about it before you ask it." Tilting his head back, he looks up at the ceiling.

"I have one. What made you want to move to Metro?"

"That is a good one. The reason is because when we moved out west, I always said that I would move back down here. Metro is the largest city in the region, and I knew that I could get a job here. That's why."

"Do you have family down here?"

"I do. In a way, coming down here is a way for me to get back to my roots and learn about my family history." Taking a deep breath, he closes his eyes.

"Do you miss your parents?" Tammy takes a sip of her water.

"I don't remember saying that you could continue to ask questions, but sometimes I do miss my parents. When I lived in Cunnings, I was a three hours' drive away from them, so if I wanted to see them, I could go home. Down here, I'm a four- or five-day drive or a five-hour flight away."

"If you had the money, would you fly back?"

"I won't fly. I'd take the train or the bus, or I'd drive."

"Are you afraid of flying?"

"No, I just like to take my time." Opening his eyes, he continues. "That's one thing with people these days. They're always in a hurry. They don't take the time to enjoy what they're doing, even when they are on holidays. It's sad to say that most people are busy doing this, that, and the other thing, and they forget to make time for themselves."

"I do agree with you. I try to make time for myself, but it's hard to do,"

"I have a busy schedule, as well. I work full time, go to school Monday to Friday at MDI, go to the gym every second day, and I still make time for myself." Grinning, he adds, "talk about busy."

"What are you taking at MDI?"

"I'm taking business. It's a four-year course done in ten months with no breaks. School starts at seven in the morning, so it's an early morning when I work all night and then do my homework."

"Charles, I don't think you have told me what you do for a living."

"I think you are right, but don't let it go to your head. I'm the line supervisor for the hotel I work at. I cook at the Tim's Hotel."

"So, tell me, why are you taking business then?"

"Because I want to leave cooking." He leans forward in the chair.

"Bad memories?"

"Not really. We just don't have time to get into it today." He clears his throat. "Back to where we were before the stupid questions started. I remember this one time when we still lived in Hillsdale. We went to my mother's parents. My grandfather and I went for a drive in the woods. We came to a dead end and he turned the truck off. We got out of the truck and walked through the woods for about fifty feet until we came to a meadow filled with black bears. He continued to walk into the meadow and I followed until we were in the middle of the bears. My grandfather then laid his hand on one of the bears and started to pet it. He told me to be gentle if I was going to do the same. Other bears came around us to see what was happening. After that experience with my grandfather, I realized that he had a touch for animals. He always told me never to fear an animal because they can pick up on your feeling and they will believe you're a threat to them."

"How old were you when that happened?" she questions him in disbelief.

"You don't believe me, but that is fine. We were still living in the house on the mountain, so I would have been about five." He looks at his watch. "Well, it's five to three, so I will see you next week." Charles gets up and walks out of Tammy's office.

"Tammy! Tammy, wake up," her boyfriend Matt says, as he lightly shakes her.

"What are you doing home so early?" Tammy responds as she opens her eyes.

"It's eleven, Tammy."

"I must have fallen asleep. How was your day?"

"It was good. Chef said that I could have tomorrow off, so maybe we could go out for dinner and then see a movie. How does that sound?" he starts to make a pot of coffee.

"It's eleven, what do you need a pot of coffee for?"

"The chef wants me to plan a new menu for the dining room."

"He gives you the day off and you have to plan a menu. It's always work with you." She throws her hands up and heads to the bedroom. "I'm going to bed. You better sleep in the living room because I don't want to be woken up by you coming to bed."

"Tammy, what did I say other than I have to do some work tonight?"

"We'll talk tomorrow," Tammy says, slamming the bedroom door in Matt's face.

CHAPTER three

It's seven Tuesday morning and Tammy's alarm is going off. Opening her eyes, she shuts it off. Rolling out of bed, she makes her way to the kitchen to put on a fresh pot of coffee for herself. After getting the coffee on, she heads to the bathroom to take a shower before work.

Tammy steps out of the bathroom and notices Matt at the table before heading to the bedroom to get dressed. Walking out into the kitchen, she gets a cup of coffee. "How long have you been up?" she questions him as she sits down at the table.

"I haven't slept yet." Matt picks up his papers from the table.

"You haven't slept yet. Well go to bed then."

"You said you wanted to talk today, so what is it?" Matt gets up from the table to get a coffee.

"We will talk when I get home from work."

"Why don't you want to talk now? It's not like you are going to be late for work." Matt sits back down in the chair with his coffee.

"Because I said that we'll talk tonight."

"Fine, then. I'm going to lie down and get some sleep." Matt gets up, leaving his coffee on the table, and heads for the bedroom.

"Are you forgetting something?" Tammy takes a deep breath to calm herself down.

"What did I forget?" Matt stops and turns around.

"Your coffee." Tammy raises her voice.

Matt walks back to the table and picks up his cup and dumps it down the sink. "Is that better?" He shakes his head and goes to the bedroom.

Tammy sighs and heads back to the bathroom to put her makeup on and to do her hair. Looking at her watch, she sees it's only eight. "Might as well go to work," she thinks. She leaves her condo and heads toward The News to get a paper. "Good morning, Rob," Tammy says, as she gets to the till.

"Good morning, Tammy, just the paper today?" Rob opens the till.

"Yeah, just the paper today."

"Well, you have a good day Tammy." Rob smiles to her.

Tammy takes a different route to her office than the day before. She arrives at the building, takes the elevator up to her office, and sits down in her chair. She opens up her paper and begins to read it.

Session Three

"Good afternoon, Ms. Maxwell," Charles comments, as he sits down in front of her desk.

"Good afternoon, Charles. How are you today?" Tammy opens up his file.

"I'm well, and yourself?"

"I'm all right. Where would you like to start today?" Tammy picks up a pen from the desk.

"I think I'll start from when I left Cunnings," Charles looks out the window. "I had just turned twenty-two. I woke up that morning and turned to my girlfriend and told her that I needed to change my life. I was trafficking drugs on top of cooking in the kitchens of the city. I was getting tired of that life style, so a change was needed. I broke up with my girlfriend, left my job and moved back home to Sova.

I was at home for about ten months before I moved down here."

"What did you…," Tammy says before Charles interrupted her.

"Hold the questions, I'm not finished. About a week after I moved home, my parents came down here for a wedding. They were gone a month which was good because I needed to dry out from city living. The first job I took was working in a retirement home as a cook. It was only a temp job that lasted a month. I then got a job in the oilfield on a steam truck cleaning oil tanks, buildings and during the winter we thawed pipelines as well. It was dirty work but I liked it. I learned fast the oilmen code of respect for the oil. The code is 'Am I coming home in a body bag today or not'. That is the reason for the respect. I remember this one day when we were cleaning this one tank. I was inside the tank that was filled with sour gas and my air supply came undone when I jumped over a riser in the back of the tank. I landed in knee-high oily sand and then realized that I had no air. I reached for my safety tank and turned it on. I then headed for the door of the oil tank. I ran out of air three steps away from the door. Those last three steps felt like a lifetime without air. I almost died that day. It made me think about how quickly you can lose your life and that we are not in control of that fact. My last day in the oilfield was on May twenty-first," Charles make eye contact with Tammy. "For those few months that I lived at home, I did make a friend. I worked with her at the retirement home. Over that time we had coffee at least two or three times a week. She listened to me as I told her my past and I did the same as she told me about hers."

"Charles, I would like to know something. How many counsellors have you had over the years?" Tammy makes a note in his file.

"I told you to save your questions. Since you asked I'll tell you. I have had five different ones since I was fourteen," Charles shakes his head back and forth.

"Did you have bad experiences with them?" Tammy takes a drink of her water.

"I did. One said that my parents were to blame; he never thought that the abuse I was going through in Prussia wasn't the reason. Another one said that my father was telling me how to answer the questions that he had given me to answer. He didn't know that I have a reading problem. The only good counsellor I had was in Cunnings. He at least listened to me and didn't follow the book. He was the counsellor at the school I was going to for cooking. The way the story goes is that on the first day of class all of us students had to write an essay about our life. So I was truthful and wrote about my life up until then. A couple of days went by and I was then asked to the office to meet with the Dean of the program. The Dean said that my instructor had brought the essay to him to read. He asked me if I would see the school counsellor. So I did," Charles looks out the window.

"I see you haven't had the best of times with psychologists. Charles, have you ever been on medication for depression?"

"I have. Now you are trying to label me. That's the biggest mistake that all doctors and psychologists make. The medical personnel then treat the label and not the patient."

"Charles, would you be willing to see a doctor?"

"What will that do for you? You'll not be able to find out what was said between us. So tell me, how would it help you?" Charles rolls his eyes.

"I feel that seeing a doctor would benefit you. I could even get you an appointment with my father."

"Do you think I need to see a psychiatrist Ms. Maxwell? Or would you like my medical history?"

"I think that seeing a psychiatrist would help and knowing your medical history would also help," Tammy makes eye contact with Charles.

"First off I won't see your father, but I will tell you my medical history. I will start with my ears. My ear canals are shaped like elbow pasta. This condition makes me tone deaf and the reason why I have a monotone voice. I had tubes put in my ears when

I was six. Other than that I have not had any other operations. I don't really get sick, but when I do it's bad. That's my medical history in a nutshell, anything else Ms. Maxwell?" Charles breaks eye contact

"No, that's all."

"Anyway, I forgot to mention that when I left Cunnings that my plan was to move down here right away. What stopped me was that I had no money saved up. That was one of the reasons I was in the oilfield," Charles closes his eyes.

"When you were working in the oilfield did you ever see it as a career?"

"No, it was just fast cash. Most of the workers in the oilfield are uneducated. That is the reason why they are there. The oil companies and the service contractors will hire anyone whether they have a high school diploma or not. They don't even care if you have a criminal record or not. All they care is if you show up for work."

"You said that you made a friend when you were in Sova, who is she?"

"Her name is Jen. She is three years older than me and is a single mother. As I said before, she was my sounding wall. She helped me realize that what happened to me in Prussia is what fuelled me for what I did in Cunnings and that it wasn't my fault. It was a case of cause and effect reaction. One person can only take so much before they lose grip on their reality of knowing what is right and wrong. She showed me a kind shoulder to cry on I guess. But she has been through a lot as well. In a way, we helped each other on getting over the past," Charles opens his eyes and looks back out the window.

"Did anything happen between the two of you?"

"No, our relationship was just friends. To be honest, the thought never crossed my mind. I would go over to her place after work and have coffee with her. The hardest thing that happened was when it was about three months before I was to move down here and she said that it would be the death of me. As the days got closer to when I was leaving, she kept telling me that it was a mistake that I was making and that I wouldn't see it until it was too late. I still talk to her at least once a week and she is happy that things are going well for me," Charles rests his head on the back of the chair.

"Do you miss her now that you are down here?" Tammy makes a note in the file.

"I do and I miss her daughter Sarah. Before I left Sova I went to her place and gave Sarah a stuffed animal. Jen said to me that day that she was only a phone call away and not to be afraid to call," Charles looks at his watch. "Look at that, it's only two thirty. I thought it was later than that. Time must be moving slow for me; that could be a sign."

"What do you mean a sign?"

"Everything happens for a reason. Maybe you will help me find peace with life or something to that effect. I'll tell you about a fishing trip that my grandfather took my brother and I on," Charles leans back into the chair. "We dug worms for bait in the morning and then we got into the truck after lunch. We drove for about ten minutes west of Hillsdale to a brook. It was normal when mom's parents came down that we would go fishing. After we got to the brook, we walked down to his favourite place to fish. We put our lines in and in about an hour we had pulled twenty nice size fish out of the brook. We started up the brook back to the truck. I was carrying the fish and I fell into the brook and lost all the fish. So I was dripping wet and when we got back to the house my grand-father told the story to everyone in the house. The lesson of the story is if you go fishing, carry money with you and know where the nearest fish market is. As well, don't get a six year old to carry the fish when you are walking back to the truck."

"I see. That is the second time you brought your grandfather on your mother's side up. What about your father's dad?"

"He died when dad was about eleven. If you mean Al, dad's step-father, we really never did anything like that other than taking us kids on the fishing boats. I don't have many memories of him. I don't even know much about his past," Charles gets up. "Ms. Maxwell, I think that we will have a short session today." He then turns and walks out of the office….

It is quarter to nine when Carolin arrives at the office. Seeing that Tammy is already there, she heads into Tammy's office and sits down in front of the desk. "Good morning Tammy."

"Good morning Carolin, how are you this morning?" responding she puts the paper down.

"I'm good. I was watching a show about the human brain and how it has evolved over the years. It said that we only use ten percent of our mind and people who suffer from mental illness use more. The other thing it said was that how the doctors have moved forward in the research into the understanding how the brain works. There was another interesting fact that the people who suffer from mental illness may not have an illness at all."

"That's news to me, that people who suffer from a mental illness may not have an illness at all. For all the years that doctors have studied people suffering from mental illness; are they all wrong with what they have found about them?"

"That's what they were saying. As well that it's all part of the evo-lution of the brain and that the symptoms are just how the brain works to counter set itself," Carolin leans forward.

"That could be, but who are we to go against what doctors say? I have to say that they have the evidence and they should know what is or isn't an illness."

"You would think so, but I think that they don't. They treat them all the same with pills and counselling. As therapists we shouldn't rule out that they could be wrong with what they see," Carolin leans back into the chair. "You know what I mean?"

"I do, but how often have the doctors made a mistake?"

"In mental health I think that they don't have a clue and they are just trying to understand what's really happening in the brain," Carolin smiles.

"You know, you should go into law because you could make anyone believe you," Tammy laughs.

"I think that would be fun," Carolin laughs. "It's almost nine so let's get ready to help our patients." Carolin gets up and walks out of Tammy's office to her desk.

The day goes quickly for Tammy and Carolin. As they are getting ready to leave for the day the phone rings. Carolin answers it. "Good afternoon," she says and then sits down in her chair and opens up the appointment book. "We have an opening for Wednesday at nine in the morning next week," she says picking up a pen. "Who is it for?" she sets the pen down on the book. "We will see you then Charles," Carolin closes the book. "Well, he is coming back Tammy."

"Who is?"

"Charles Davis, he will be here next Wednesday at nine. I only wonder what is going to happen next. Want to go for coffee?"

"Not tonight, Matt is off so I will be at home and if he isn't there I will give you a call and we will go for that coffee," Tammy locks the door as they leave the office.

"Sound like a plan," Carolin says to Tammy as they walk down the hall to the elevator.

"I'm thinking that Matt will have supper ready. Hopefully. If not, we will be going out to eat because I'm not cooking."

"I wish you luck then tonight. Remember try not to get into a fight with him. He has been good to you over the last three years that you two have been together. He just has become busy with his work and all you need to do is remind him what is important."

"That's the thing. I think that he thinks that I will always be there. I can't take him working all the time. I want to have children in the future and I want a man that will be there for them."

"If I don't see you tonight, I will see you in the morning," Carolin turns to the right as they walk out of the building.

"See you later, Carolin," Tammy then and heads home.

As Tammy walked down the street all she thought about was what would be at home when she got there. There was a distant thought of Charles, but not enough to take her mind off Matt and what she was going to say to him. Getting to the door of her condo she takes a deep breath in and opens the door. "I'm home," Tammy sits on the stair and takes off her shoes.

"Supper will be ready in a few minutes," Matt yells from the kitchen.

Tammy walks to the other bedroom that she and Matt are using for an office and sits down in the chair in front of computer. She turns on the computer and checks her email. "Matt, what's for supper?"

"Stuffed chicken with a roasted red pepper cream sauce," Matt walks into the office.

"So, what time did you get up?"

"I was woken up at two by the phone."

"Who called?" Tammy knew in the back of her mind it was his boss.

"It was Chef. He wanted to know if I was done the menu and if I could work tonight because one of the line guys called in sick," Matt walks back into the kitchen.

"I hope that you said no," Tammy walks into the kitchen.

"I did or I would be at work now," Matt checks the rice and vegetables that were on the stove. He then pulled the chicken out of the oven and set it on the front burner. "Supper is ready." Tammy gets a plate and dishes herself up. She then gets a glass of wine and sits down at the table. Matt does the same and sits across from Tammy. "How was your day?"

"It went well and I have an old patient coming back next Wednesday."

"Who is it?"

"Charles Davis, he called at five just before Carolin and I were out the door."

"That's good. So you said that you wanted to talk, what's up?" Matt takes a drink of his wine.

"Where do you see this relationship between us going?" Tammy makes eye contact with Matt.

"What do you mean Tammy?"

"What do I mean? I mean, where are we going?" she breaks eye contact with a sigh.

"I think that we are on the right track for the future. You have mentioned kids and I think that would be good when we are ready. You have mentioned marriage and it is time that we settle down."

"That's what you see. I see us going towards a break-up to tell you the truth," Tammy puts her fork down.

"Why do you say that?"

"You're never here and when you are here you are always working on stuff for work. I sit at home every night alone when you are at work. It's to the point where I don't know if my boyfriend even cares about me anymore."

"I do care. If I didn't care I would have left the relationship a long time ago. I'm sorry if that is the way you feel," Matt takes a deep breath.

"If you do care, you would choose me over your job."

"You want me to choose between you and my job? What am I supposed to do for work?"

"We have had that discussion before. You can go to school. You can work almost anywhere and if you do go to school you wouldn't have to worry because I do make enough money to pay all the bills and then some. Matt, I don't want to lose you but if you don't do something about that job, you'll be out the door. This is the last time that we are going to have this talk because there will be no next time," Tammy gets up from the table. "Do you really want to lose me? I'm going for a walk. Think about it because when I come back, you better have a decision."

Tammy walks over to the door and slips on a pair of runners. She opens the door and walks out. Shutting the door she heads down to the waterfront.

Session Four

"How are you today Ms. Maxwell?" Charles says as he takes a seat.

"I'm all right. And how are you today?" Tammy asks him as she opens his file.

"I'm doing well. I guess I will start today from when I was eighteen," Charles turns and looks out the window. "My grad was over and it was summer. A few months earlier my parents told me about a family reunion in Highlow, which is about five hours north of here. It was mom's parents' fiftieth wedding anniversary as well so they thought that they would have all the family there. We left a couple of days after my grad and my sister came with us because my brother was going to fly down. I was not feeling that well, so the drive was a long four days. When we got to Highlow it took my grandmother to tell mom and dad to take me to the doctor. The doctor told me that I had an inner ear infection. So I was sick the whole time that I was down here. Back to the reunion, it was down at the camp site, which was a good five-minute drive from my grandparent's house. I saw how different I was than the rest of the family. It made me think that I was adopted. After that, I made a decision to walk back to my grandparent's house. I told no one where I was going, so to make it short, the family all were scared that something happened to me. The family all started to search for me. I was found by my grandfather when I got to the house. He told me that everyone was looking for me but he said that he knew that I would go to the house and that is why he stayed there."

"Charles, have you had problems with your family?"

"It's not that I have problems with them, it's that I'm the black sheep in the family," turning he makes eye contact with Tammy.

"Does that bother you?"

"Not really, it just means that I'm different from everyone else," Charles clears his throat.

"Have you always thought that you were different than everyone else in the world?"

"Isn't everyone different from each other? I am different, the things that I have gone through in my life makes me different. Are you not different from me?" questioning Tammy he leans back into the chair.

"I am, but we are the same too. We are both human and have had experiences that have shaped us in different ways," tapping her pen on the desk she only wonders where he is going with this.

"You're full of stupid questions and stupid answers today. You didn't really think about that one did you? Anyway, you were saying that we are the same as well. I think that your judgment is off. We're not the same and I can be sure of that fact," he shakes his head in disbelief.

"Charles, why don't you tell me about Prussia then?"

"You want to hear about Prussia, the town where I was hated? Do you know what the meaning of hate is? Don't answer because I will tell you. The meaning of the word is to dislike intensely. This is the meaning from the dictionary. When I first moved there the people were nice. Then I started school and the story was different. It took about a month before I was a target for everyone. This was when I knew I was different from the rest of them. The teachers took me out of the class at that time and put me in a separate classroom, which didn't help matters. The bullies attacked me like I was a lone wolf. For the ten years I was there I was mentally and physically harassed. I've been beaten down with boards and anything else they could grab to use as a weapon. They even threatened to kill me a couple of times. I never let them break me down even when there were seven or eight of them attacking me. I would always get back to my feet and I would swing again. I'd never back down no matter what," turning back to the window, he continued, "I never let my parents know what was happening to me. Then one day my sister saw me getting beat down by some older kids as a teacher stood watching, letting it happen. That was the day my parents found out. They came to the school and talked to the principal. To be honest I was called to the office and heard my parents yelling at him. After about ten minutes I was called in. Let's just say that's when my parents threatened legal action against the school. The principal then became very concerned for his job and acted. After that meeting things changed for a couple of weeks and then it started all over again. I was in grade eight at the time. Then one day I was attacked by twelve of them and nearly beaten to death. I spent the next two weeks in the hospital after that. When I got out of the hospital, mom and dad took me up to Toon and I bought a boot knife for protection. The Monday that followed I stabbed one of the bullies that had put me in the hospital. I followed him into the bathroom. I stabbed him four times in the back and he was hospitalized in Toon for three weeks as doctors had to save his life."

"How did that make you feel when you stabbed him? I know that it's a stupid question, but I want to know."

"It felt good. I got him back for what he was part of and each time I knifed him I asked him how it felt," turning, he makes eye contact. "I'll tell you this; after he got out of the hospital he tried to get the other students to stop bullying me. He wasn't the leader of them but I sent a clear message to the rest of them. You know, when you beat someone close to death and a month later that person stabs you, it makes you think twice before doing anything like that again. After the stabbing I thought he would finger me but he didn't. Everyone knew it was me, even the teachers. They couldn't do anything to me because they couldn't put me in the bathroom when he was stabbed. I was on a free class and so was he, so no one knew where we were. Ms. Maxwell, I have a question for you. Were you ever bullied in school?"

"No I wasn't. I was one of the popular girls in school," Tammy answers as she makes more notes.

"So you were the one who thought her crap didn't stink. Great, I have a princess as a counsellor," he shakes his head once again.

"I wasn't one of them, I had my friends and we spent most of our time in the library."

"Did you go to a private school Ms. Maxwell?"

"I did, does it make a difference?" rolling her eyes knowing that he was going to say something.

"It does. In a public school the rules are different from a private school. In public school you only pay a small amount of money because the government pays the teacher. In a private school the parents of the students pay the teachers. Anyway, the teachers in Prussia knew what was happening to me but since we were not from town they turned a blind eye to it," closing his eyes he continues, "When I was in grade nine my parents said that if they could afford to put me in private school they would but it never happened."

"Are you mad at the teachers for turning a blind eye to the abuse that you were going through?"

"I am. I have ten years of emotional scars on me from Prussia, not to mention that many years of built up anger. Let's just say it takes a great deal of strength to keep it under control. I'm afraid of my anger because I never have lost control of it," then he opens his eyes. "All I can say is that Cunnings would have been different if I hadn't gone through that abuse in Prussia."

"I don't think that it would have been that different if you went through the abuse or not. The reason is because you would have had the same choices. So why would it have been different?"

"It would have been, you'll understand when I talk about it," turning away from the window.

"Charles what else happened in Prussia, if you don't mind me asking," Tammy takes a sip of her water.

"A lot happened. Every day if I wasn't running when school ended, I was beaten up, so you can see the reason for the knife. If I was out for a walk or bike ride I always had to look over my shoulder, but I knew where I could go after a year or two. I was like a prisoner in that town. I was happy when dad got the job in Sova because I knew that I was leaving Prussia. Another thing that I learned in Prussia was not to trust anyone and I'm still like that," turning back making eye contact with her. "We could talk for hours about Prussia, but we are going to change topics. So Ms. Maxwell, ask away."

"Charles, how long did you live in Cunnings?"

"For four years and in that time I moved four times. The first place I lived was the U of C dorms. That lasted until January tenth. I was kicked out for throwing the floor coordinator down a flight of stairs after he started something that he couldn't finish. After that I lived in a basement apartment three blocks away from the school I was going to. After I finished school I moved downtown off of Jasper Ave and one hundred and fourteenth street. The last move was to a different apartment in the building."

"Why did you throw the floor coordinator down the stairs?" making a note in the file and underlining the word violence.

"I told you, he started something that he couldn't finish and he was drunk. The fall only broke his leg and he hit his head a few times but he lived," resting his head on the back of the chair and he looks up at the ceiling.

"What did he do to make you use such force?"

"He was calling me down and then he took a swing at me. I grabbed his hand and threw him down to the floor. I asked him if he was finished and he said yes. So I let him back up, then he hit me and I put him down again putting my knee on his throat. I asked him the same thing and he said yes. I got off him and started towards my room when he tackled me from behind. I got up and put him in a headlock and walked him to the stairwell. I used his head to open the door and I threw him down the stairs. I hope that has answered your question."

"It has. Charles what were you taking in school when you were in Cunnings?"

"I was taking Culinary Arts, in other words cooking. I like the first one better because cooking is an art form."

"Well, how long have you been cooking for?" bring her hand up to cover her mouth as she sneezes.

"It all started when I was eleven. I was having a reaction to some food I had eaten and dad decided to take me to work with him. I was sitting in one of the chairs watching T.V. at the nursing home. Then the cook came over to me and asked me if I wanted to make cookies for the residents. I said sure and that is where it all started. I volunteered there until I was fifteen when I got a job at a local restaurant called Billy Bob's. After getting that job the bullies attacked me even harder. I think it was the fact that I was making my own money," running his hands through his hair he continues, "I remember the following summer because the owner of Billy Bob's left so I, at the age of sixteen, got another job with a local farmer hauling grain and bales for him. When school started up the job ended. That September a new couple moved to town and re-opened the restaurant and they gave me a job. I worked at Rattlers until I moved to Sova."

"Kids can be cruel," Tammy said tapping her pen on the desk.

"That's an understatement Ms. Maxwell, as I said before I dealt with it for ten years. They weren't kids, they were animals. Anyway, back to cooking. When I moved to Sova I got a job cooking at the Sova Motor Inn. I worked there until I was finished school."

"Charles, were you bullied when you lived in Sova?"

"Only once through the whole year. The bully in the class on the first day thought he had fresh meat but he was wrong. I broke his arm when he went to hit me. I then had to go to the office and they soon found out what I had been through in Prussia. The teachers understood and I only missed the next day of classes. The good thing about it was that the bully and I saw eye to eye after that," he chuckles.

"Charles, last week you said that you want to get out of cooking, so I want to know why?"

"Don't get me wrong, I love cooking but it has the highest average for alcohol abuse, the second highest in suicides, drug abuse, stress and failed relationships. There are other reasons but we just don't have time today," looking at his watch he continues. "We have time for one more memory from when I lived in Hillsdale. My mother's parents came to visit. I have always loved trains so they took me to Hillsbro to where they had train rides up the river. When I got to go on the train I felt like I was in heaven. I'll see you next Monday at two." Charles gets up and leaves.

An hour had passed before Tammy returns home. As she opens the door she could hear music playing. Walking in she took off her shoes and heads to the living room where Matt was sitting. "So do you have an answer for me?" Tammy sits down on the sofa.

"Tammy, do you really love me?" Matt turns the music down.

"Yes I do," looking over at him trying hard not to cave in.

"You do. I only wondered because if you did you wouldn't make me choose between you and my job, that's all," getting up and he walks into the kitchen to fill his coffee cup. He returns to the living room and sits back down. "I would never expect you to decide between me and your job."

"Why do you say that?" she questions him with annoyance in her tone.

"I say that because when you get mad at me it is always about my job. For the whole time that we have been together, I have worked nights. I have always been there for you, time after time. What difference does it make if I am cooking or not?" "What am I going to say to our kids when they ask where you are?" Tammy raises her voice. "Am I going to say that Daddy loves you but he is working and that's why he is never home? Really Matt!"

"Tammy is this about kids that we don't have yet?" calmly he tries to keep his cool.

"No, it is about you and me."

"Tell me then what do you have against my job?"

"You make thirty thousand dollars a year and you work fourteen to fifteen hours a day. They're taking advantage of you! That's what I have against your job," Tammy starts to cry.

"I'm a Sous Chef, what did you expect when I took the job?"

"If you work a normal job you would be making more or at least working eight hours a day," she continues to cry.

"So what you want is for me to quit my job and start out at the bottom again making no money or go to school and put myself in debt. Those are some great options you are giving me Tammy," he makes eye contact with her.

"Matt, stop," she wipes the tears off her face.

"Stop what? The truth of the matter is I can't afford to go back to school or start at the bottom again. My parents didn't pay for my education. I did. Not like you. I have had to fight for everything I ever got so far in life. You have had your schooling and that office paid for by your parents. I didn't grow up in a family with money," he starts getting madder.

"Matt please, I love you," she starts crying harder.

"It's the same thing every time I have a day off, we get into an argument about something and it always ends with you crying. Do you think there is a problem here? I try Tammy, I do. I think it's time for you and I to get some help, I really do. I do love you but you make it hard sometimes. I never question the decisions that you have made in your life so why do you question mine?"

"Because I love you and I want the best for you," Tammy pushing out through her tears.

"If you do love me you wouldn't try to change me. Love me for who I am, not what you want me to be," getting up out of the chair he walks to the door and opens it. Walking outside he sits down on the step to get some air to calm himself down.

About a half hour had passes before Tammy goes outside. She sits down beside him, "Sorry. I just wanted you to get out of cooking."

"Tammy, it's who I am and I can't change that. You know that my father is a chef and it didn't bother me when I was growing up. When he had days off, he was with my sister and I the whole time. It's not the amount of time spent together but the quality of time. That's why I don't like fighting with you. I know that you get lonely when I am at the hotel until all hours of the night and I know that it bothers you but you have to see it my way too. Over half of the guys that I work with can't hold on to a relationship because the women in their lives don't want someone who is always working all the time. Three years ago we were roommates and when we started going out you were OK with it." Matt looks at Tammy. "Listen, if I didn't love you I would have been gone a long time ago."

"I know." She leans her head on to his.

"Tammy let's get some shoes on and go for a drive." Getting up to his feet, he heads for the front door.

"Sure. Let's go to the lookout down on Bay Road."

As they drive out to the lookout, they talk about their dreams and the future. When they got there, they walk along the rocks to a point where they could watch the sunset over Metro. After the sunset, they head back to the car and drive back to the condo. On the return home Matt goes into the kitchen to make a pot of coffee.

"Matt it's almost ten at night, what is the pot of coffee for?"

"I was just getting it ready for the morning," he starts pouring the water into the coffee maker.

"I see, well I going to get ready for bed," she heads to the bedroom.

"I'm going to take a shower and then I will be in there too."

About a half hour passes before Matt goes into the bedroom to find Tammy asleep. He then sets his alarm for six and sits down on the bed. Laying his head on the pillow he drifts off to sleep.

CHAPTER four

It's Wednesday morning and Matt's alarm is going off. He reaches up and turns it off. Rolling out of bed, he makes his way to the kitchen to turn on the coffee maker. After a quick shower he wakes Tammy up, and then gets dressed for work. "Tammy, there is coffee on. I don't know what time I will be getting off work tonight but I will try to be home by seven," Matt then heads back to the kitchen. He rinses out his plastic coffee mug and pours half of the pot of coffee in it. He places the lid on it and picks up the papers that have the new menu. Walking down the stairs to the door, he puts on his boots and leaves the condo.

About five minutes pass before Tammy makes her way to the bathroom to get ready for work. After she is done in the bathroom, she makes her way to the kitchen to fix herself a cup of coffee. Walking back to the bedroom, she dresses and does her hair and makeup. She makes her way out of the bedroom, sits down in the living room, and turns on the TV to the news channel.

After Tammy watches the news until eight, she gets up and walks over to the stairs. Looking down, she sees Matt's papers on the step. Thinking nothing of it, she walks by them and puts on her shoes. She then picks the papers up and heads out for work. Instead of walking the normal way to work, she heads over to the hotel where Matt works, just down the street from her office. As she enters the hotel, she heads into the restaurant and walks over to the window of the kitchen. She asks the cook to get Matt. As Matt walks over to the hot pass of the line, Tammy says holding up the papers. "You left these on the step."

"Thanks, Tammy. I had just started looking for them." Matt takes the papers from her.

"I'll see you tonight." Tammy walks out of the restaurant and gets to the street heading to the office building, which is only three blocks from the hotel. She stops by a newsstand on her way to get a paper for the office and a bottle of water.

It is 8:40 when Tammy arrives at the office. She unlocks the door and walks in. Making her way to her office, she sits down in her chair and begins to read the paper. Ten minutes pass before Carolin gets to the office.

"Good morning, Tammy. How are you today?" Carolin sits down in one of the chairs in Tammy's office.

"Not too bad today. How are you?" Tammy puts the paper down onto the desk.

"I can't complain. Had a run-in with an ex-boyfriend last night during my walk." Carolin leans her head back on the chair.

"Oh, how did it go?" Tammy leans forward, putting her arms on the desk.

"Well, he introduced me to his new girlfriend, who was dressed like a hooker. I was happy to see that his taste has changed to the gutter tramps," Carolin laughs. "How was your night with Matt?"

"We had a fight and I left the condo for a walk and then when I got back we fought some more." Tammy turns to look out the window. "He, well, we have to get some help or our relationship will fall apart, if it hasn't already."

"I can help you two," Carolin smiles.

"You are one of our friends. Not to say no, but we need to see someone that we don't know. You know what I mean?" Tammy stands up and walks over to the window.

"I understand. It would be a conflict of interest because I see you every day and might see Matt once in a blue moon. Would you like me to find someone for you this morning?" Carolin relaxes her head on the chair and looks up at the celling.

"That would be a good idea. Then I will call and make an appointment." Tammy turns to face Carolin.

"I'll do that for you," Carolin says, and walks out of the office.

Session Five

"Good afternoon, Charles. How are you today?" Tammy smiles and makes eye contact with him.

"I'm all right. So, let's talk," Charles takes a seat.

"That sounds like a good idea. Last week, we were talking a little about your past in Prussia, some about cooking, and a couple other things. How about we continue with those things?" Tammy opens his file.

"We will have time for that another time. I think we will talk about suicide today. What do you think about that?" Charles shows a half grin.

"We can talk about that if you want." Tammy writes "suicide" down in his file.

"In most religions, taking your own life is wrong because God, or whatever you want to call Him/Her/It, has put you here on earth for some reason. So with that in mind, does that mean that you go to hell when you die?" Charles turns to look out the window. "Ms. Maxwell, I asked you a question."

"Oh, I thought you were going to speak more. I would think so." Tammy takes a deep breath.

"I see. We will leave religion alone. Anyway, April is a hard month for me because I had two friends kill themselves. Have you ever had that happen to you?" Charles turns back to make eye contact with Tammy.

"I haven't, Charles."

"So you don't know what it feels like then? The guilt, the pain, and the never-answered questions of could I have helped or not." Charles closes his eyes, then continues. "Rod Blake was two years older than me. I met him when I moved to Cunnings. He was my roommate when I lived at the university dorms. We became friends quickly. He was going to school to become a doctor. Everything was going well for him and his family is well off. I always wondered why he lived in the dorms. After I left the dorms, we remained friends. March came around and then I got a call from him wanting to know if I would go for coffee with him. So we met in one of the trendy coffee shops in downtown Cunnings. I think it was the March 27 when this happened. Getting back to the story, he told me that he had seen a doctor who said that he was suffering from depression and started him on anti-depressants. I didn't think much of it because the way I thought at the time was that the doctor knew what he was talking about. Rod said that the doctor also mentioned that he should see a counsellor, and once again I thought the same thing. What I didn't realize at the time was that Rod seemed happy and at peace with himself. I found out after that most people who kill themselves are happy and at peace with themselves once they have made the decision to really do it. For the whole time I knew him, he was never at peace with himself, and I should have picked up on it. He told me that if he killed himself, he would leave my name and number on the suicide note. I laughed because I thought it was a joke. He said that he was heading to his parents' on the first of April." Charles opens his eyes and made eye contact with Tammy. "On the third of April, I got a phone call from his parents telling me that they found Rod dead. They said that the suicide note told them to call me. You want to know how that makes me feel?"

"I don't need to ask because I think I know. What did you do?" Tammy makes a note.

"Nothing. I remember getting a cold chill up my spine and then I went numb. I sat down in the chair that was beside my phone as his mother cried in my ear. That call came at two in the afternoon. Let's just say when I went to work that night I saw myself not caring about anything in my life. So tell me, Ms. Maxwell, would that affect the way you thought about life?" Charles turns back to the window again.

"I feel that it would change the way you would think. How do you deal with it?" Tammy takes a sip of her water.

"I'm still dealing with it. As I said before, I had two friends commit suicide. I'll tell you the story of Kevin Reese. He was my other friend who did himself in." Charles lowers his head. "I met Kevin in the dorms, as well. He was three years older than me and lived on the floor above me. He was studying to become a teacher. To make this story short, I will leave out some things. His upbringing was that of a middle-class working family. We would talk at least once a day and we would go for coffee at least once a week. He knew Rod, but wasn't one of his friends. Kevin killed himself one year and fourteen days after Rod, two days before my birthday. I remember about a month before that, Kevin had been going through some tough times. His parents separated in December, his grades were not good, and his uncle was murdered. In a way, he was under some stress, or that is the way I saw it. In January, he started using drugs. I remember that because he asked me to get him some." Charles makes eye contact again.

"On April 17, I got a call from his dad telling me that he was dead. My name and number were on the suicide note. His dad said that he found Kevin's handgun on the desk, but he didn't put a bullet in his head. He had found a few ounces of cocaine beside him. Kevin must have thought to get high and then do himself in."

"What went through your mind, Charles?"

"I was in shock that he'd never said anything about suicide. I was still trying to get over Rod's suicide, and then his happened. That's when I started to smoke weed, to help me deal with their deaths. Two friends kill themselves in the span of a year. I felt like giving up after that." Charles rubs a tear from his eye.

"Do you still smoke weed?"

"No, now I take a moment every day to ask God to forgive them for taking their lives. Thinking about their suicides now brings back all the memories of them and the things I was doing at the time when they happened. All the feelings I had when I got those phone calls and everything else. You know, whoever came up with the line that suicide is painless has never dealt with it, or has used that line to disconnect themselves from the fact. I don't know. It is painful for the families and friends who have to live on after the suicide." Charles clears his throat.

"Just by the look on your face I can tell that it was hard for you to tell me that." Tammy brings her hand up to her mouth.

"You should try living with those memories. I can still remember the sounds of their parents' voices when they were telling me the news. That is a sound I will never forget or want to hear again." Charles closes his eyes. "I'll tell you something, Ms. Maxwell, just to change the topic for a minute or two. Out of all the children who get harassed by bullies, fifty percent will commit suicide. Another twenty-five percent will go into the crime world to inflict the pain they suffered as a child onto others. The remaining twenty-five percent will fall into a deeply depressed state and avoid human contact as much as possible. Those who commit suicide will sometimes take someone else with them, and it's normally the bully. That is the scary thing these bullies don't know. I was reading in the paper the other day about a school shooting. What happened was that this kid took his dad's gun and went to school and hunted down the bullies who picked on him. He got three and then took his own life." Charles opens his eyes.

"Did you ever think of doing something like that when you lived in Prussia?" Tammy taps her fingers on the desk.

"I told you last week what I did."

"Charles, have you ever thought about ending your life?"

"I was getting to that." Charles runs his hand over his eyes. "I almost fell into the fifty percent of bullied kids. The first time was when I was seventeen. It happened in early June. The year before, in October, my Dad's stepdad side passed away. After that, my father lost his job in January. I was in grade eleven and I was still having problems with the bullies. They knew that there was something happening in the family, so they had fresh information to attack me with. Mom and Dad left on the tenth of June to visit the family down here. Five days later, I drove my bike about five miles down the highway to the train tracks. I turned onto the tracks and went down the line another mile. I set my bike on the embankment away from the tracks. I then lay down across the tracks and waited for the train to come. As the train approached, I could feel the rails shaking. At that moment, I said my last goodbye to the world. Then out of nowhere, I felt pressure on my back, like someone lifting me up. The next thing I felt was hitting the dirt and the wind from the train going by me. I don't know what it was, but whatever it was, it didn't want me dead. I went back home and sat down on the chair in the living room. About an hour later, the phone rang. As I went to pick it up I noticed the number was not one I knew. I picked it up and the person was looking for my dad. When I told him that my parents were down here, he asked me to get my dad to call him back. In short, that person is now one of our family friends and what he wanted to tell Dad was that the health board in Sova was offering him a job."

"Charles, did you have a suicide note? If you did, what did you do with it?"

"I kept it and put it in a safe place where only I know where it is." Charles looks to the floor.

"What do you think moved you off the tracks?" Tammy taps her pen on the desk.

"I don't know. Maybe the hands of God." Charles turns to look out the window. "That was the first time I tried, Ms. Maxwell."

"How many times have you tried?"

"Three times in total. The second time was after Kevin's suicide. I walked out onto the top of the High Level Bridge and was ready to jump. At that moment, I blacked out and came to at home. The third time was a few months later, and the same thing happened. Someone or something doesn't want me to die." Charles starts to shake his head.

"What caused you to get to that point in Cunnings?"

"I was giving up on life. I had a bad childhood, I was involved in the crime world, and I was having trouble dealing with the suicide of my friend."

"I guess you fell into another percentage area for bullied children."

"I did. Let's just simply say that I got into the crime world about two months after I moved to Cunnings. That's for another day." Charles makes eye contact.

"Have you thought about killing yourself since you moved down here?"

"Not really. I'm learning to deal with things in a different way. You can't run away from your problems because when you stop, they are always waiting for you." Charles looks at his watch. "Ms. Maxwell, have you ever tried to commit suicide?"

"No. Why do you ask?"

"So you don't know what it is like. Most people who have tried to kill themselves for the first time and live will keep trying until they do succeed. There is help, but it doesn't normally work because most people have their minds set on death. After the first time, I didn't think about it again because I changed the way I was thinking. With the last time, I walked down the streets of Cunnings thinking about life and what I wanted and, well, it has worked so far." Charles closes his eyes.

"Charles, I hope that I will be able to help with getting over your past,"

"You know, if you keep making assumptions, you will be the one needing mental help." Charles smiles. "How about I tell you a story?"

"Sure," Tammy says and puts the pen down.

"Well, this one is about life. This story happened many years before my time, some 2,000 or 3,000 years ago. The way it goes, is that a child of God was born to a young woman and it was a boy. As the boy grew, he started to preach the true word of God. All the other religions in the area heard what he was saying and they wanted him dead. When he was thirty-three, he was brought out to the public square and killed in front of his followers. What the meaning of that story is to me is that people don't want to hear the truth, much like today. The collective mind of mankind has not changed since then. It is sad to say. We have advanced by leaps and bounds but still are afraid of the truth. Ms. Maxwell, it is three so I will see you next week." Charles gets up and leaves the office.

The morning goes by quickly for Tammy and Carolin. At lunch, they make their way to the Public Gardens to eat. Carolin turned to Tammy as they sit down on a bench. "I think you and Matt should take a holiday together. You both have been working straight for three years. Maybe that would help the situation between you two."

"It might, but what do I do about our patients? We are booked up to the end of September." Tammy takes a bite of her sub.

"Well, go for the holiday then."

"I don't know if Matt and I can wait until then." Tammy looks to her left.

"Get away for a weekend then." Carolin raises her eyebrows and makes eye contact with Tammy.

"You know, you are not making this easy."

"Well, I just want to help. I only want the best for you guys." Carolin looks over to the pond where a swan is swimming.

"You know, swans mate for life, and that is what I want with Matt. I would do anything for him, Carolin. Did you find a number for me?" Tammy looks over to the pond.

"I did and then I called him. His name is Tim Oaks and he said to get you to call him today sometime." Carolin gets up from the bench and looks at her watch. "We should go back because it is getting close to one."

"I guess so." Tammy also stands. They exit the Gardens and walk across the street and into the office building. As the elevator doors open, they walk in and Carolin pushes the button for their floor. The doors close. "I'll give Tim a call when we get back to the office, so you will have to give me the number."

"Not a problem, Tammy. That's what friends are for." The doors open and they walk over to the door of the office. Carolin opens it, goes over to her desk, and picks up the phone number. "Here it is, Tammy."

"Thanks for this, Carolin." Tammy takes the number from Carolin's hand. Tammy walks into her office, sits down behind her desk, and picks up the phone to call the number. "Hello, could I talk to Mr. Oaks? Yes, I'll wait."

"Good afternoon, Tim Oaks here."

"Mr. Oaks, this is Tammy Maxwell. A friend called you this morning and told me to give you a call."

"How can I help you, Tammy?"

"It's my relationship with my boyfriend. I feel that we need help." Tammy leans back in her chair.

"What I can do is have you come in for an appointment. We can talk about some things and go from there. How is five tomorrow for you?"

"That sounds fine. Thank you." Tammy hangs up the phone and walks out of her office over to Carolin. "Can you get me the address for Tim Oaks's office?"

"His office is on the eighth floor of this building. It's not that far from here."

"What did you do to find that out?" Tammy sits on the edge of the desk.

"Easy, there is this thing on the main floor that has the names of the businesses in the building on it. But I asked when I was talking to his receptionist this morning," Carolin laughs.

"I guess you got me there," Tammy says, and then walks back to her office.

Session Six

"How are you today, Charles?" Tammy asks as Charles sits down.

"I'm fine. You know, Ms. Maxwell, since I started coming here, you have never asked me how my week was. That is a good question to ask because life happens during the week. But who am I to know anything about counselling? You know that I question your methods and you never thought to ask me a simple question like that. Those are the types of questions that help build a good relationship, and they show that you care a little about how my week has been. You must have been asleep or not listening when they covered that topic in class," Charles laughs and makes eye contact.

"So, Charles. How was your week?" Tammy breaks eye contact.

"It was fine. Next question," Charles says, turning to looked out the window.

"It was fine, that's it?" Tammy asks, shaking her head. "All right, if you want to play like that, then you won't have a problem telling me about the harassment you went through in Prussia."

"Ms. Maxwell, I'll tell you more because you asked nicely. Well, I went through ten years of it, but you already know that. It was ten years of hell, and that's the reason I tried to commit suicide the first time. There is only so much that one person can take before those thoughts pass through their mind. When we moved to Prussia, I was seven. I started grade three and I thought that the kids were the same as me; however, I found out differently. After a month of class, I was separated from them. The teachers and the school felt that I needed one-on-one help for my reading, so I was moved to a different classroom. In the new classroom, there were other kids there that were older than me who were getting help for other classes. I was in there all day, every day. A month went by before they started doing tests on me, including an IQ test. They never told me what the results of the tests were in grade three, but they informed my parents. The school did tests on me again in grades seven and ten. On the last IQ test in grade ten, I asked the teacher what I scored and I wanted to see the mark for myself. She showed me and, at that time my IQ was 155, so it's not low by any means.

"During the breaks during the day at school I would leave the safety of the room and the students would attack me—at first verbally, then physically. Let's just say I learned how to fight over those ten years." Charles clears his throat. Taking a deep breath he continues. "The teachers knew I was being harassed, but they just turned a blind eye to it. My parents found out what was happening when my sister witnessed it firsthand. After that, Mom and Dad came to the school. But it only made it worse. I shouldn't say that because there was two weeks that followed my parents' visit when everyone was afraid to do anything to me. Ms. Maxwell, do you know what the meaning of the word 'harassment' is? No need to answer, because I'll tell you. It means to torment."

"Charles, children can be so cruel. I wouldn't blame you if you never forgave them. What happened to you in Prussia was wrong; no one deserves that." Tammy looks at Charles. "Not to try and change topics, but what do you see out the window?"

"Everything, Ms. Maxwell. I see everything," Charles closes his eyes. "So, do you still want to talk about Prussia? It wasn't much fun for me."

"If you want to, Charles. I can see that the memories of Prussia are painful for you, so it's up to you." Tammy makes a note in the file.

"I'll continue. I did make a friend there, but we haven't spoken in years now. I think the last time I talked to him was when I lived in Cunnings. Anyway, his name is Terry. He is a year older than me.

Terry was like another brother to me. I remember that we would go bottle picking on our bikes, go fishing, and do other things that we enjoyed. I miss him; I only wonder where I messed up our friendship. I would like to say that we grew apart, but I know different. Ms. Maxwell, that chapter of my life is over and it's hard to remember it because all the memories come back to life and play over in my mind again and again. It feels like I just moved to Sova again from Prussia. I still have the pain and hate inside of me and it's killing me slowly. What I experienced in Prussia was hate and that was all." Charles opens his eyes. "You said children can be cruel. They weren't children; animals, I would say. What I went through there has scarred me for life. Ten long years of memories that haunt me every day and I wish never happened. I exploded and released my rage in Cunnings. We will get to that in the future." Charles turns his head to make eye contact. "You asked me how my week was."

"I did." Tammy breaks eye contact again.

"The best time to ask that question is at the beginning of the session, but it was good. I had a call from my parents the other day and they asked me how this was working for me. Work went well, other than there is one person that I work with who needs help more than me, but he is normal. Go figure. As well, I never told you that I live with two women on the corner of Morris and Birmingham. It's about a five-minute walk from here. One of my roommates has the same name as you and the other's name is Shannon, a stupid blonde. Anyway, things are good and I hope that this week will be as good as the last.

"Ha, I'm crazy. I can go from talking about my past and then to something that really doesn't matter at all," Charles laughs. "You know, I would not wish for what happened to me in Prussia onto anyone's child. The only downfall is that it happens every day in places all around the world."

"That's true and it's sad that it happens. I remember when I was in public school, there were bullies in the first grade."

"So, you were in public school. When did you go to private school? I hope you don't mind my asking." Charles leans back into the chair.

"I started grade four in the private school."

"Your parents should have kept you in the public school system. The reason I say this is because you would be able to understand your patients better." Charles moves his head and attention to the window. "You missed the lesson that public school would have taught you. However, all schools are the same. They say they shape your mind, but really they manipulate everyone to think inside the box. If you think outside the box, they'll hinder you with questions. You should already know this. The students that don't fit into the box, they separate them from the rest, which makes them an easy target for the bullies. What I just told you is something that no teacher would ever teach or even tell you. That is the way that today's society works. If you don't fit into the box, you are labelled with some type of mental illness. If you take us away from society, the evolution of the human civilization will stop. Another thing no schoolbook or teacher will ever tell you. Do you understand me or do you need a program? In other words, are we building a relationship or not?"

"I do understand what you are saying and I think that we are slowly building a relationship. Charles, you can call me Tammy if you want. For the last few weeks, I've been waiting for you to lower your guard some. I can see that you are starting to let me into your world. You seem to be a good person who has had a difficult life. I can see that you are not depressed, but in pain from what happened to you in your past." Tammy takes a sip of her water. "I think that I have to see through your eyes to be able to feel your pain."

"See through my eyes. Why don't you just walk a mile in my shoes? I know that you would only get about a step before you'd break down and cry. I'll have to teach you how to see. Amazing, this will be the first time that I'd be teaching a counsellor something." Charles shakes his head and continues, "Tammy, if I have to teach you how to see, then you have to listen to my words. I will paint a picture in your mind. First, close your eyes. Allow everything to become black and quiet. Now, see yourself at the age of seven. You and your family have just moved to a new town in a different part of the country. You're different from the rest of the children and you don't fit in. For the next ten years of your life, you are harassed daily. How do you feel. Or do you feel anything?"

"I feel like the world is against me and that I want to leave. I now understand why you tried to kill yourself." Tammy opens her eyes. "Charles, how do you hold yourself together?"

Charles slowly turns. "It's hard, Tammy. I don't trust anyone anymore and I'm not sure what keeps me from going off."

"Charles, I understand,"

"You don't. I live everyday like that. That might be the reason why my boss thinks I need help. Every day since I have left Prussia I have kept a journal. That was August 15 1996, in the same year as my seventeenth birthday. It didn't matter that Dad and I were living in a tent trailer behind the old hospital in Sova until the end of the first week in September. However, I still don't trust anyone, not even you, Tammy. Maybe someday, but you will have to prove to me that you are trustworthy."

Charles looks at his watch. "It's that time again. What story do I want to tell you today? We'll go with this one. My grandfather would tell me his stories from the war that he was in when he was in his twenties. He was a tank driver and he was going through a village and saw a starving dog. He stopped the tank, got out, and gave the dog some food. At first, the dog showed its teeth. Then it sniffed the food, approached my grandfather, and took the food from his hand. For the rest of the war, that dog was part of the tank crew. It allowed my grandfather and the other members of the crew to sleep during the night. The meaning of the story is that if you take a moment to be kind, you will be rewarded.

Anyway, it's three; I'll see you next week." Charles gets up from the chair and leaves the office.

As the last patient leaves the office at 4:30, Tammy walks out of her office with the file. "Here is Gail's file." Tammy places the file on Carolin's desk.

"Thanks, Tammy." Carolin picks it up to put it away. "So, did you get a hold of Tim? What did he say?"

"I did. He wants to see me at five tomorrow afternoon." Tammy sits down in one of the chairs in the waiting room.

"What are your plans tonight?"

"Nothing too much. Matt said that he would try to get off by seven tonight, so nothing till then."

"Would you like to go for coffee then?" Carolin turns her computer off.

"Sure. Do you want to go to Mark's?"

"That's where I was thinking. I just have to pull the files. Well, that can wait till the morning. Are you ready to go?" Carolin gets up and starts to the door.

"I am." Tammy follows Carolin out the door and locks it.

As they enter Mark's, it begins to rain. "I'll get a seat before they are all taken. Order for me, Tammy." Carolin takes a booth near the window.

Tammy gets the coffees and makes her way to the booth. "Good thinking, Carolin, to get us a booth."

"You know, Tammy, there are many counsellors who seek help for things in their life." Carolin makes eye contact with Tammy.

"I know. I hear the problems of our clients all day and I help them with those issues. I think that if we as people keep everything inside, we will eventually lose ourselves and fall down. I try to get our patients to talk about what is bothering them and most of them talk about other things in their lives." Tammy takes a sip of her coffee.

"Maybe the things they are talking about are related to the problem, and that's why they feel that telling you about those things is where their problem emanates from." Carolin looks out the window.

"That's possible. I just think that we need to wake up and walk forward and forget about the past." Tammy taps her fingers on the table.

"The past is what makes us who we are, so to forget the past is to forget what made us…. But I know what you mean." Carolin watches the rain hit the window.

"The past is what makes us, yes, but to live in the past is not healthy. Everyone who seeks professional help felt that their past is the worst and most of them have had a hard life and they dwell on it. They don't see the light at the end of the tunnel and they have lost all hope in life. They feel that everything that happens is negative, and they never look at the positive in the situation."

"This is true and it is easier to find the negative in life than the positive. It's like you with Matt. You are only looking at the negative things in the relationship. How does he make you feel? What kind of things does he do for you? You know what I mean?"

"I don't look at the negative things in the relationship. They just outweigh the positive at the moment." Tammy looks away to the door.

"See? You are. Over the years, I have always looked for the positive in every situation, even when the lesson that was being taught was hard to take. You are like a sister to me and I want you to be happy. For the last few weeks, you haven't been yourself. I hope that Tim can help you." Carolin sips her coffee.

"What do you mean that I haven't been myself?"

"Well, you haven't been the Tammy that I have known over the years. For the last few days, after your dad talked to you, you have been on edge, and after I told you that Charles was coming back, your mood changed."

"It's just brought back memories of three years ago and what was happening in my life then."

"Stop living in the past then. Live for the moment and only for the moment. You can't change the past because that is behind you and the future hasn't come yet, but we can shape it. At this moment, it is raining outside and we are having a coffee. That is the moment we are in, so don't look back but look forward." Carolin smiles.

"I guess you are right, live for the moment." Tammy finishes her coffee. "Have you ever walked in the rain because you wanted to?"

"I have and I still do. I normally put on my old, torn blue jeans and my university tee shirt and walk until the rain stops."

"It has been a long time since I did it. I think that the last time was with Matt." Tammy looks out the window. "The rain has stopped. If we make a break for it now, we can get home before it starts again."

Tammy and Carolin make their way out of Mark's and then head to their homes. As Tammy gets home, she sits down in her living room and turns the TV on to watch the six o'clock news. After that, she makes supper for herself. She sits down at the table and sees that it is seven o'clock. She hears the door open as Matt gets home from work.

"I'm home," Matt says, as he closes the door behind him. He sits down on the stairs and takes off his boots.

"How was work today, Matt?"

"It was fine. And your day?" Matt walks up the steps and heads to the kitchen.

"It was a day."

"That's good. Chef has asked me for a beer, so I will be heading out for a few hours. I just wanted to tell you like this instead of on the phone." Matt heads to the bedroom to change.

"It wouldn't have mattered." Tammy lowers her head slowly, trying not to let it affect her.

"See you later, Tammy." Matt goes down the stairs to the door. He puts on his shoes and leaves.

CHAPTER five

It is Thursday morning and Tammy's alarm is going off. Getting out of bed, she puts on her housecoat and walks out to the kitchen to make coffee. She looks into the living room and sees Matt sleeping in one of the chairs. Walking over to him, she wakes him up. "What time did you come home last night?" She gives him a light kick to the leg.

"Around one." Matt slowly gets to his feet.

"Why did you sleep out here?"

"I didn't want to wake you." Matt walks into the wall.

"You must be still drunk. Coffee is on and you have to get ready for work." Tammy walks back to the bedroom to get dressed.

Matt goes to the kitchen and pours himself a coffee. He sits down at the table only to fall back to sleep.

Tammy finishes getting dressed and makes her way to the bathroom to get ready for work. Seeing Matt asleep at the table, she walks over to him and kicks the chair he's in. "I'm leaving in five minutes, so get ready for work." Tammy goes to the kitchen and fills up her to-go coffee mug.

"I'll see you tonight if you are not working all night or out getting drunk."

"It was one night, give me a break." Matt walks to the bathroom.

"And last week and the week before. You come home drunk every night that you work. At least you are walking and not driving." Tammy raises her voice.

"So you call me drunk when I only have three drinks." Matt slams the bathroom door.

Tammy shakes her head and then heads to the front door. She sits on the step, puts on her shoes, and opens the door. Looking up the stairs, she takes a deep breath and leaves.

Tammy walks up the street to The News to get a paper before work. Rob smiles as she approaches the till. "Good morning, Tammy. Just the paper today?"

"Yeah, and can you check my ticket?" Tammy hands the ticket and the money for the paper to him.

"Good news, you get to play again. Hopefully, the next time it's the winner." Rob smiles again.

"Well, maybe I will play again when the pot is a big one. That way, if I win I will give you half and we can both retire together." Tammy smiles back.

"That sounds like a good idea, but I will still own this news store and work here. Tammy, have a good day, and we will see you tomorrow morning."

Tammy makes her way out of the shop and heads to the office. Once there, she sets down the paper, turns on the coffee pot, and begins to read. She notices that it is twenty-five minutes before she looks up from the paper. She walks out of her office and gets herself a cup of coffee.

A few minutes go by before Carolin shows up for work. "Tammy, are you sick? This is two days in a row that you have gotten here before me," Carolin says, walking into Tammy's office.

"No, I'm fine. Matt and I had a small fight this morning, so I left before it got out of hand." Tammy puts the paper down.

"What was the fight about, if you don't mind my asking." Carolin sits down.

"He went out drinking last night after work." Tammy leans back in her chair.

"Tammy, the thing about relationships in this day and age is that you can't try to change them. You have to allow him to live his life and you have to live your life. The most important thing is that you accept him for who he is." Carolin makes eye contact.

"You're defending him. He drinks every night when he works, what would you call that?" Tammy clears her throat.

"I'm not defending him. I'm just saying that you shouldn't try and change him. If he drinks a few every night after work to relax, there shouldn't be a problem as long that he isn't coming home drunk. It is the lesser evil of all the choices that are out there. Would you rather he was doing hard drugs?" Carolin gets up from the chair.

"You know that I dislike people who drink and I really dislike people who use drugs." Tammy looks up to at Carolin.

"I know the story that you are about to tell because you have told it to me several times. Tammy, that is in your past and your uncle can't hurt you anymore. I think that everyone has a drunk in his or her family." Carolin walks over to the window. "You know, Tammy, my father used to drink after work until he was drunk all the time. I watched as he poisoned his body and it killed him in the end, but I don't hold that against him. If my brother or I had something important, Dad would be there and he would be sober."

"I know, I'm just under so much stress lately and I don't know which way I'm going. I think that is what is causing everything to be bigger than it is." Tammy picks up the paper again.

"It's almost nine and we have a full day today." Carolin walks out of the office to her desk in the waiting room.

Session Seven

As the clock strikes two, Charles walks into Tammy's office and sits down in the same chair as before. "Good afternoon, Tammy."

"Good afternoon, Charles. How are you doing today?" Tammy opens his file.

"I'm fine. I had lunch at Rocks on the Rocks today. Anyone who likes good food would love that place." Charles makes eye contact. "That was some storm that we had last night and to think it is only May. It's nice to see that the sun is out today to dry up all that rain. Anyway, let's start talking about my four years in Cunnings." Charles smiles and turns to look out the window. "But, first, I want to remember when the Trade Towers came down to the ground. I was asleep and it was my day off when my mother woke me up to say that jumbo jets had hit the Trade Towers in New Amsterdam. I didn't believe her until I saw it on the TV. The date was September 11. I remember thinking that after everything that that country has done to the world, dropping the atomic bomb, imposing its will by threats on countries that can't defend themselves, it has made itself the bully of the world and I feel that it deserved it. It was an act of desperation by the countries that were being pushed around. You would think that the lesson being imposed would have been seen. The only thing that happened was that two defenceless countries got bombed and invaded because they felt that the men behind September 11 lived there. The funny thing about it is that they wonder why almost every country on the planet dislikes them and you know who I mean. Anyway, Cunnings."

Charles looks toward Tammy and then back to the window. "I'll call the four years in Cunnings 'the dark years' because that's what they were. I did manage to get my papers in cooking so that would be the phoenix of those years. I have no idea how I did it, but I did. It was the fifteenth of August when I moved up to Cunnings. I was eighteen and I was going to pursue my love for cooking. I was enrolled in college for culinary arts. "So far, it's not that dark yet. I had good intentions when I went there, but the anger that I had built up from Prussia was a ticking time bomb that was ready to explode. Let's say I met the wrong people and they became friends. Logan and Jay, I met them when I went to a social that the University of Cunnings was putting on. Logan, a six-foot-six black man from New Amsterdam in his final year in business administration, was working as security at the function. He looked at me and said, 'Come here, white boy.' So I walked over to him and told him to take a hike. He then grabbed me. 'You should be careful who you say that to. Your sister used to go to school here. Your name is Charles if I'm not mistaken?' I asked him how he knew my name and he told me that my sister asked him to watch out for me and to be a friend. He then introduced me to Jay, who was white and finishing his degree to be a druggist." Charles smiles and looks back at Tammy.

"Charles, that doesn't seem dark or stressful. So you met some people; that is what happens at gatherings." Tammy writes down the two names.

"They were only the beginning. I am socially inept, and meeting new people is hard for me. I didn't know what to say or do when Logan was introducing me to his friends and, well, he started me on smoking weed. It wasn't the people I was meeting, it was one person who brought the hate in me out. Her name was Kelly, my first girlfriend. She was a law student in her third year at the university. I met her through Jay. Anyway, she invited me out one night to her parents' place in the west end of the city. We were maybe dating three weeks. So I went over to meet her parents and to have supper with them. Her dad, a big-shot lawyer, asked me about a hundred questions which I think is normal, but the answers I gave must have impressed him because he invited me into his den for a drink.

"'Charles, do you drink scotch?' he asked me, as he poured two shots into a rocks cup for me. I said that I didn't drink much. He then said, 'Well, when you are here, we will have a scotch together.' I said, 'Sir, that sounds like a fine idea.' We talked some more and then he asked me if I wanted to make some extra money. As a student with a shoestring budget, some extra money always helps. So I said that I would do it before he told me what it was.

"I will tell you some more about Sir. He was not only a lawyer, but part of an organization called The Ghosts, which I'm still part of. He was, or most likely still is, the western president. The Ghosts are in the crime world, and are feared by all other crime cartels on earth. That isn't the only place we are found. We are politicians, doctors, lawyers, police officers, judges, business owners, and just about everything that can be done we are there. The job he offered me was to run large quantities of drugs to drug suppliers in the city. For the next few years that followed that night, I was running drugs. I don't know how I held onto jobs or much less how I finished school. I got Logan and Jay into it, as well. The three of us became a team, with me being the leader. Thinking about it now, I was stupid to get them involved in that world." Charles takes a deep breath.

"So the running of drugs was the 'Dark Years.' That doesn't seem so bad," Tammy says, leaning back in the chair.

"No. There were more things that happened than just delivering drugs. There was violence involved. I have been shot at and, yes, I returned fire. I had no problem beating someone down if they didn't pay up to send a message that we meant business. I was releasing the anger I had inside me and I didn't care how many people I hurt. As well, every night I wished that I would be killed by someone."

"Are you still part of that world?"

"No. I'm still a Ghost and you can't leave once you are in. I became an inactive member after I left Cunnings. Sir knows that I'm down here and I have the numbers of the leaders of the Ghosts who are down here. Cunnings was a long time ago now, and I have to live my life. I will tell you more about Cunnings later." Charles turns to make eye contact.

"Charles, are you still the person that you were in Cunnings?" Tammy takes a sip of her water.

"I hope that I have changed since then, but if in that situation again, I would probably turn into the same monster that I was then. That part of Cunnings is over and I'm done talking about it." Charles breaks eye contact.

"I'm sure that we will talk about it more in the future." Tammy makes a note in the file.

"Maybe, but don't be so sure of it. The other side of Cunnings was my cooking. I went to school to get my papers and I started to work in hotels in my second year. I made some friends in school, one being Chris Davies. One night, I was getting ready to quit cooking and he took me aside and told me that if I was going to quit, I should quit everything. He gave me a wake-up call. To tell you the truth, Tammy, I don't want to talk about Cunnings at all. It's four years of my life that I'll never have again and there are painful memories, as well. Maybe in later sessions I'll talk more on it." Charles turns to look out the window.

"What would you like to talk about then?" Tammy runs the end of her pen down the file.

"Let's keep it simple. Something like how my week has been." Charles leans back into the chair. "I had a call from my brother and we don't get along, so I only wonder what the dolt was trying to prove. At home, my two roommates have been fighting nonstop. I have tried to play peacemaker a few times, but it doesn't seem to work. So yesterday, Shannon, or stupid blonde, left with her boyfriend and then there was peace in the flat. I found out Friday from my boss that he is giving me a better position with more responsibilities, and I'm looking forward to that promotion. In my spare time between work and life, I have been writing. That, for the most part, is how my week has been going." Charles closes his eyes.

"Charles, you said that you and your brother don't get along. Why is that?"

"We haven't got along since I was in Cunnings. He came up for a visit and found out about my activities in the drug world. He went home to Toon and called me up and told me that I was a bad person and that I was letting the family down for doing it, but not that nicely. Since that day, I have never cared if he lived or died." Charles opens his eyes.

"That's not good then. Have you tried to make peace with him?"

"No, and it won't be happening anytime soon. When I moved out here, my first night was at his house and he told me that I better not get involved in that world again." "Well, let us change from that topic, but I feel that we should make sure we try to fix the relationship with him. You said that you write in your spare time—what kind of things do you write?"

"I write poetry and essays. As well, I write a journal every night." Charles looks at the time on his watch. "We're just about out of time. Is there anything you want to know before I leave today?"

"There is. You said that you see differently. Could you show me how you see?" Tammy sets down her pen.

"So you want me to teach you how I see? I thought I showed you that last week, but I guess you forgot. First thing is that you have to close your eyes." As Tammy closes her eyes, Charles continues. "Tammy, now that your eyes are closed, clear your mind of all thoughts. If any thought comes to you, label it 'thought' and let it go. Do this until your mind is clear. After clearing your mind, allow yourself to relax by taking a few deep breaths. Now picture a place that is peaceful for you. Tammy, now let the energy from the heavens come down in a white light and cover you from head to toe. Feel the peace within you."

Charles goes silent for a few minutes before he continues. "Now, let the picture go black and then open your eyes." Tammy opens her eyes. "That's how you see. Do you understand me now?"

"I think so. I saw the place like as if I was there. Who taught you that?" Tammy makes eye contact with Charles.

"There is a story that goes with it. My Aunt Brenda was the person who taught me that. The story goes like this: I was turning twenty and my cousin Andy was getting married. I drove down to

Pen, which is a thirteen-hour drive southwest of Cunnings in the mountains. I'd finished my shift at the hotel at midnight and got in my car and drove all night. I got to my cousin's house and crashed on his sofa in his living room. I woke up after my Aunt Brenda shook me. Anyway, we talked and got onto the topic of spiritually. She told me that this little exercise would help me relax and clear my mind. Once you understand how to relax, your vision will change. You will then be able to see the truth for what it is and you will understand what is happening around you." Charles smiles.

"I see. It was a cute trick. How many people have you done that to?" Tammy picks up her pen and makes another note in the file.

"More than one and less than a million. I'll show you something else maybe, but not today." Charles gets up from the chair. "I'll see you next week," he says, and walks out of the office.

As Tammy and Carolin sit down for lunch at the restaurant on the main floor of the building, a waiter brings them water and menus. "Could I get you ladies a drink to start?"

"I'll have a coffee." Tammy picks up the menu.

"The same for me, with cream and sugar." Carolin smiles at the waiter and picks up the menu, as well. The waiter leaves the table to get their drinks. "Tammy, I was thinking this morning between patients. In this day and age, we have everything that we could wish for. We have phones that take pictures that are connected to the internet, and that is only one example."

"Yeah, what is the point you are trying to get at?"

"Ready to order, ladies?" the waiter asks, as he returns with their drinks.

"I'll have the chicken pesto pasta." Tammy hands the menu to the waiter.

"And I'll have the apple-smoked pork salad." Carolin closes the menu and hands it to the waiter. "Going back to what we were talking about. The point that I'm trying to make is that technology is changing the way we live our lives, but is it good for us?"

"I think that it is. We all have to evolve one way or another." Tammy fixes her coffee.

"I think that we do have to evolve, but spending billions on technology is the wrong way. If they would put that money into the homeless, let's say, we could get rid of that problem that plagues the streets of almost every city." Carolin takes a drink of her coffee.

"We could do that; however, that's not the world we live in. The way most governments on this planet think is that socialist ideals are meaningless and, well, the war machine is what drives technological advancements."

"That is true in theory, but look at the countries that are Communist. Everyone has health care, a job, and a place to live."

"They do, but they don't have the freedom of speech or the choice of how many kids they want. Communism is a great idea on paper, but it doesn't work." Tammy turns to look out the window. "Even look at the socialist countries. They may have freedom of speech and free health care, but they have their problems, too."

"Tammy, we live in a socialist country and it is a lot better than a capitalist country," Carolin says, as the waiter brings the food.

"Thanks." Tammy continues. "Carolin, there are good things about all forms of government, and on the flip side of the coin there are bad things, too."

"Maybe one day there will be a New World Order and only one government to govern the world." Carolin takes a fork full of salad.

"To comment on what you just said, it was tried and it failed. How does this conversation have to do with anything, anyway? We went from talking about technology to politics. We should be talking about the advancements in the treatment of the mentally ill." Tammy starts to eat.

"Tammy, the treatment of the mentally ill hasn't really changed in hundreds of years. The only difference between the treatments now and then is there are more drugs to use on the patients. They still do electroconvulsive therapy, which is passing electricity through patients' bodies and then doping them up on drugs. That is what is happening in the mental hospitals around the world. Then they set them free without guidance other than a suggestion to see a counsellor if they want help. The patient loses their grip on reality again and ends up back in the hospital mental ward. That's the kind of system we work in. If the government really wants to research something, it should look at mental health, because it affects us all in one way or another."

"You know, the treatment isn't the best but we are further ahead now than we were a hundred years ago." Tammy takes a few more bites of her lunch.

Session Eight

"Good afternoon, Tammy." Charles sits down in his chair. "Oh, may I take a seat?"

"You may. How was your week?" Tammy flips open the file to a blank page.

"You're learning; that's good. My week has been going well. I got a phone call from my parents the night before last, and they told me that they were planning a trip down here in a few months. Work is going well and my boss is happy that I'm coming here for this support. At home, the girls are fighting again, so I'm looking for a new place to live. For the most part, I'm spending my free time down at Mark's drinking coffee and writing. Other than that, nothing is really happening in my life at the moment." Charles looks out the window. "You know, Tammy, I'm writing a story around our meetings. I've put you and Carolin as friends and that you are living with a man that I call Dean. The funny part of it is that you want a relationship with him." Tammy's jaw starts to drop. "And then the patient took the session to another level, but his name is not Dean."
"What did you say?" Tammy tries composing herself.

"You heard me. I said that I was writing a story and you are the star and all I am is a supporting character. See what happens when you write? You have the ability to look into a person's eyes and see what they are truly hiding from. So who holds the pen?" Charles makes eye contact. "Did I hit a nail on the head or am I off?"

"No, it's just amazing how creative your mind is. Do you draw?" Tammy breaks eye contact.

"Sometimes, I do, when I can't put it down in words. You know, that question was a little stupid, but you have to ask them to know what type of artist a patient is." Charles reaches into his jacket pocket. "Would you like to hear something that I wrote the other day?"

"No, but I'll read it." Charles hands Tammy the piece of paper. She opens it and begins to read. "Charles, that's very deep. Is this how you write?"

"With my poetry, anyway." Charles gets up from the chair and walks over to the bookshelves. "Very interesting, these books you have." He pulls out one of the old textbooks. "However, they only teach you what other doctors and such have experienced with their patients over the years." He puts the book back and returns to his chair. "Maybe you could get more information from the comic page of the local paper on mental illness than from those books. At least the people who write the comic strip have a closer understanding with their public than the doctors who wrote your textbooks," Charles laughs.

"It's just a killer that the education you got and you still don't have a clue on how to deal with patients. You should go back to the school and ask for a refund." Charles turns to look out the window. "If you're wondering what my point is, it is that they teach you about the illness and how to treat it.; they don't teach you how to help the patient emotionally. This is the truth for the medical field. No time to help and they send the patients to people like you who have no idea what is happening in the person's head. Doctors only treat the illness and not the person, and an appointment with them is fifteen minutes long, so how do they know what is really wrong? I wonder how much a doctor makes off those fifteen minutes. If they only took the time to get to know their patients, the trust and respect would return back to them. The same also goes for people like you."

"Charles, why is it that you say that?" Tammy runs her finger down the page of the file.

"I'll tell you. Look at the world we live in. It's full of money-hungry people. No one has time for anyone else anymore, even for their families. I'll tell you a story. For the four years I lived in Cunnings, I saw all the sides of this world that we as people live in. One day, I was walking to work and I passed a homeless person on the street. I asked myself, if I were on the street and homeless, would anyone give me the time of day? The answer I came up with was no, because people only care about themselves and how they can get the next money fix. So, I turned around and walked over to him. I said hello and gave him some money. He said thanks and I went back on my way to work. As I walked, I looked at the things that I had: a place to live with food in the kitchen and a family I could fall back on if I needed it. I realized how much I had and it sickened me." Charles shakes his head and continues. "The down-fall is that he could have been hooked on the same drugs I was trafficking. So, Tammy, look at Metro and tell me if it is not the same as Cunnings? Down here, I'm not in the crime world, but I have a job, a place to live, food in my apartment, and a family to fall back on. Metro has homeless people, the drug world, and other crime. It sounds the same, doesn't it?"

"All cities have the same problems; some more than others."

"You missed the question. The question was about the fact that people don't care about one another anymore. People only care about their income of money. You have to start paying attention to what I'm saying to you a little better," Charles closes his eyes.

"What do you think should happen then?" Tammy rolls her eyes.

"What do I think? Well, I'm one man and poor; who would listen to me?" Charles opens his eyes.

"It was a poor person who cried for change and it happened."

"I've got a colourful past and for me to say something could get me in a lot trouble, if not dead." Charles opens his eyes and makes eye contact before continuing. "You know, I'll tell you something. Life happens and the rich will always hold down the poor. It has been that way for years. What the rich don't want to hear is that, throughout history, the poor have always fought back. There are more poor people than rich, and all it takes is a movement to start, and that is starting to happen. History always repeats itself—remember that."

"I think it's time for a new topic."

"Does that topic make you afraid of the poor? If you want to change topics, we will. How about fate, or will you get afraid again and want to change to a new subject?" Charles smirks.

"What do you mean by fate?"

"Your fate." Charles turns to look out the window.

"My fate? What are you trying to say?" Tammy writes a note in his file.

"Well, the fact that you will die and as you take your last breath, the last thing you will remember is me."

"Do you think a lot about how to mess with people's heads?"

"I don't think about it, I just know how to do it. Trust me on this one, because I'll change you forever. You won't be the same because you're already dead and this is just the memory you have of me playing itself out. Or are you just asleep and this is nothing but a dream that you are having?" Charles laughs.

"We're alive and we're awake." Tammy looks down and writes down the word "disillusioned," and circles it on the page.

"That's your mind playing tricks on you again. That's why, when everyone gets to the final seconds of their life, they try to hold onto it. It's known that the brain is still active after death and, well, no one knows why. However, there is an upside to death and that is the afterlife and the chance that you will be born again. So, don't worry; you're at heaven's gates and I'm judging you." Charles smiles.

"How do you know this?" Tammy then prints the word "egocentric" and circles it, as well.

"Well, it's easy. I'm the oldest soul at some 60,000 years old, and you're much, much, much younger than me." Charles makes eye contact.

"How do you know that I'm not older than you?" Tammy puts her pen down.

"It's in your eyes, and they don't lie. Just to let you know, I read tarot cards, palms, and a few other things. So I see thing in a different way." Charles leans back into the chair.

"So then you can read my future. Why don't you do that?" Tammy takes a deep breath.

"Read your future? I have read your life story from beginning to end." Charles rubs his head.

"Charles, that is quite enough! How is your relationship with your family?" Tammy picks up her pen.

"I must have got you scared again," Charles laughs, and then he turns to the window. "To answer your question, isn't that easy for me. I'm the black sheep of the family. The relationship with my brother isn't good at the best of times. The reason it is the way it is starts in Cunnings. He called me one day from his house to tell me that he would be coming up for a visit with a couple of his friends. The good thing was that it was my day off from the hotel, but I was still busy with the other part of my life up there. In short, he found out about my involvement in the crime world. They left a few days later to return home and, when he got there, he called me. He told me I was a bad person and a disgrace to the whole family, like I told you before. It took my friends to hold me down so that I wouldn't drive the six hours to his house to put a bullet into his head.

"So, anyway, when I was moving down here, I spent my first night with him and he told me not to make the same mistake down here. What a prick, and I told you that last week. The relationship with my sister got better after she left to go to university. Like a good wine, it has aged well. What I think happened in our relationship, is she saw her little brother was growing up and making his own mistakes and learning from them."

Charles scratches his head. "I think that I've told you that I'm the youngest in the family. So, with that in mind, the relationship with my parents is hard to explain. For the most part, every choice I've made in my life has been questioned or deemed wrong by them. Secondly, they treat me like I'm still a little kid. You can fill in the rest with whatever ideas you have," Charles turns and makes eye contact. "So, Tammy, do you have any brothers or sisters?"

"What does it matter if I do or don't?" Tammy breaks eye contact.

"Well, I was wondering how would a person like yourself be able to understand their patient who has a problem with a sibling if they don't have any siblings? So, could you answer my question then?" Charles looks at his watch.

"I'm an only child." Tammy closes his file.

"The hour is up, I'll see you next week." Charles stands up.

"Wait a second, Charles." Charles sits back down. "What is it like having an older brother and sister?"

"During good times, it is like having two best friends, and during the bad, it's like having the other side of the coin. You can choose your friends, but not your family." Charles stands up again. "I can tell you're having a problem seeing through my eyes, but I'll tell you one thing: never say that you understand, because no one ever does. See you next week." Charles turns and walks out of the office.

Tammy finishes up her paperwork and takes it out to Carolin. "It's ten to five. You should go up to Tim's office and get ready for it." Carolin takes the files from Tammy. "I'm going to finish up and I'll see you in the morning."

Tammy walks out of the office and over to the elevators. Tammy gets on the elevator and pushes for the eighth floor. The doors open and Tammy gets off. Turning to her left, she sees the office for Tim Oaks. She takes a deep breath, opens the door, and walks into the waiting room. She sees a young lady at a desk and walks up to her. "My name is Tammy Maxwell and I have an appointment."

"Are you a new patient?" The lady looks up from the computer.

"I am."

"All right, just have a seat and Tim will be right with you." The lady picks up the phone.

Tammy turns and walks over to one of the seats and sits down. She looks beside her to see a desk that has magazines on it. The cover of the top one reads, "Mental illness is not an illness but the evolution of the human brain." Tammy goes to pick it up when Tim walks out of his office with one of his female patients. He picks up a file and approaches Tammy. "Tammy, right this way," he says, and turns to walk into his office.

Tammy gets up and follows him. Looking around, Tammy sees blue painted walls, a globe on a tall stand in one of the corners, beanbag chairs, and a coffee table in the middle of the room. In the east-facing window, there is a dreamcatcher. "This is a lot different from my office," Tammy says, making her way to a beanbag chair and sitting down.

"I find that if you make the space peaceful and relaxing, your patients will feel relaxed. I see that you must have a different style just by the way you are dressed. You're more formal and professional." Tim sits down in one of the beanbag chairs. "How can I help you today?"

"Well, I don't know where to start," Tammy says in a quiet voice.

"How about you tell me what was happening that made you call me." Tim sets the file on the table.

"My boyfriend and I are having problems. It's like he isn't caring about me anymore."

"What does he do for a living?" Tim pushes his glasses up.

"He is a cook."

"He is a cook. That means when you are at work he is sleeping ,and when you are home, he is at work. Am I right?"

"I wish that is how it was. He gets up about an hour before I do and leaves for work. He doesn't get done work until around eight or nine, and then he sits in the bar in the hotel and has a few drinks. Sometimes, he is totally drunk when he comes home and, other times, he comes home when he is done work. When we talk, he tells me how much he loves me and what I mean to him. I just don't know if I still believe him or not anymore." Tammy starts to sob.

"Tammy it is OK to cry. You are feeling bad and I can see that. Love is not one of those things that is always perfect. It's a gamble at the best of times because you are trying to make it work and sometimes there are bad times but they will pass. How long have you been with him?" Tim smiles.

"About three years." Tammy covers her eyes as the tears keep falling.

"I think that three years is just the beginning of a long-term relationship. You have to tell him how you feel and you need him to do the same. With what you have told me, he does tell you how he feels. One thing to think about, don't get into a fight by talking to him. If you think that will happen, write it down on a piece of paper and have him read it. Try that, and see what happens." Tim stands up.

"That's it?" Tammy looks up to him.

"No, come back tomorrow at five and we will talk some more." Tim opens the door. "After you," he says.

Tammy walks out of the office. "Thanks, Tim."

"I'll see you at five." Tim smiles again.

Tammy makes her way home and makes some supper. After eating, she sits down in the living room and turns on the TV to watch the evening news. About an hour passes and she starts to think about the magazine headline that she had read in Tim's office before drifting off to sleep.

As nine o'clock hits, Matt comes home from work. Taking off his shoes, he can hear Tammy snoring in the living room. He picks her up and puts her to bed.

It's Friday morning and the alarm clock is ringing. Tammy slowly gets up and turns it off. She places her hand on Matt's chest to feel him breathing. Looking to see that his eyes are still closed, she gets out of bed and makes her way to the kitchen to make a pot of coffee. She then jumps into the bathroom for a shower. As she is getting out of the bathroom, Matt is making his way out of the bedroom dressed and ready for work. "Do you remember me taking you to bed last night?" Matt fixes himself a cup of coffee as Tammy places her hand on his back.

"No, I don't." Tammy turns and heads to the bedroom to get ready for work.

"I got home at nine and you were snoring up a storm, so I thought I would put you to bed." Matt makes his way to the table to gather his mind for work.

"You could have wakened me up."

"I thought about that, but I figured that if you woke up in my arms, it would be romantic." Matt picks up one of his food magazines on the table and opening it.

"Matt, where do see us going?" Tammy sits down beside him.

"What's that?" He looks up from his magazine.

"You and me." Tammy puts her hands on his lap.

"Tammy, I love you. We just have to hold on for a few months until everything calms down at the hotel. Then I will be able to spend more time with you," Matt says, looking Tammy in the eyes as a tear forms. "Listen, I know that this is hard on you. I only wish that there was some other way for us, but I'm a chef at heart. My teachers in culinary school always said that once you're a chef, you're always a chef. You may leave the kitchen, but you will always return back to the kitchen in one way or another."

"That's all good and nice, Matt. I wish that we could be together more than the hour before we go to work or the hours when I come home after work on your days off." Tammy tries holding back her emotions.

"Tammy, we will find a way to survive. This time last year, it slowed down at work. I was getting out of the kitchen by six and home by six-thirty." Matt sets the magazine back down on the table.

"It's slow for three months, but that is when you are working on your food competition stuff because it is during that time when it happens." Tammy gets up from the table. "I'll see you tonight if you aren't too late coming home from work." She then walks down the stairs, puts on her shoes, and walks out, closing the door behind her. She makes her way up the street to The News to pick up a paper. As she is on her way up to pay for the paper, she sees the magazine that was in Tim's office. She picks it up and opens it to the related story that was backing the cover.

"Good morning, Tammy. The paper and the magazine today?" Rob smiles as Tammy approaches the counter.

"Yeah." Tammy looks up to Rob and then goes back to reading.

"That will be $10.50 today." Rob says, his finger on the top of the magazine.

"Sorry, Rob. It's just that this story is interesting." Tammy pulls out the money from her purse.

"There's another one in there about just schizophrenia." Rob takes the money.

"You have read this magazine?" Tammy asks, shocked that he might have.

"I do have my masters in psychology and this store is my office. I help people by giving them reading material and a smile. Have a good day, Tammy." Rob smiles.

Tammy smiles, turns, and walks out the door to the street. As she starts to walk toward her office, she turns her head to The News and then turns back to see where she's walking, almost hitting a light pole. She gets to her office at eight o'clock. Sitting down in her chair, she continues to read the article on mental illness.

As Carolin gets in for the workday at half past eight, Tammy is reading the article that Rob mentioned. "How is it going today, Tammy?" Carolin walks into the office and sits down.

"Not bad. You should read this." Tammy hands the magazine to Carolin.

"Mental illness isn't an illness, but a mutation." Carolin sets the magazine on the desk. "So how did your meeting with Tim go?"

"It was helpful. He wants to see me again today." Tammy looks out the window. Turning back to face Carolin, she asks, "How are you today?"

"I'm good and glad it's Friday." Carolin leans back in the chair.

"That makes two of us."

"How are you taking the news that Charles Davis is coming back?"

"He is just another patient. Speaking of which, we should get ready for today." Tammy takes a sip of her water.

"Sure, he is just another patient. Tell me why you have pulled his file then?" Carolin gets up from the chair to head to her desk in the waiting room.

"I just want to reread his file before he gets here."

"Sure," Carolin picks up the magazine and leaves Tammy's office.

Session Nine

"Good day, Tammy. How are you?" Charles sits down in one of the chairs.

"I'm good, and yourself?" Tammy picks up her pen and opens his file.

"It's another day above ground and I'm breathing, so in the grand scheme of things, I'm fine. The only downfall is if I was having a bad day, no one would care—or would they? Over the last eight sessions that we have had together, I have only touched on the surface of what I have lived through. I think that I can go a little deeper with you because I feel that I can trust you." Charles leans back and continues. "I can let my guard down and trust you."

"Thank you, Charles. I am someone who you can trust. So, tell me about your week."

"The week went well. Nothing really happened. My parents called me. Anyway, to the real reason why I'm here." Charles smiles and turns toward the window. "I can remember the short seven years that I lived in Hillsdale. It was like a dream to me. We lived on the mountain in a house that was as old as the community and it was the first house that Mom and Dad bought together. Before I was old enough to go to school, Mom and I would take walks into the backwoods to pick berries and apples during the summer and early fall. During the winter, my brother, sister, and I would toboggan down the hills around our house on the weekends and, when they were in school, I would make snowmen. I remember that day when I was going to grade one for the first time. I walked down the driveway with my brother and sister to wait for the bus. When the bus got there, my brother and sister got on. As I was following them, the bus driver told me to turn around as my mom was taking my picture. If that snapshot could talk, it would probably say that this young boy was scared and not ready for that life-changing moment. I didn't know what to expect from school.

I knew all the kids in my class from kindergarten, so I shouldn't have been scared. To this day, I still remember them all.

"Grade one went by like a flash, and then that summer hit. Mom and Dad had bought a new house near one of the rivers that runs through the village. So that was the first time I moved. Then grade two started and it was fun. I was happy to be in school. Come to think of it, that was the only two years I enjoyed school. In the January of that school year, Dad got his job in Prussia. My perfect world changed that summer." Charles takes a deep breath and continues. "You know, Tammy, the one thing about time is that it moves forward and we get older. If I only could turn the hands of time back, I would freeze them when I was in Hillsdale. I would still have my innocence."

"What do you mean, Charles?" Tammy takes a sip of her water.

"Just as I said, I was liked and had friends." Charles closes his eyes. "I don't blame my parents for what happened to me in Prussia. It was like the hate that I endured was meant to happen to make me a stronger person. I didn't deserve it though. I remember being beat down with two-by-fours by five or six kids. Before grade six it was pushing, shoving, and name-calling, and then grade seven started and I began to fight back. That was when they started to beat me. I had to run home at lunch and after school because I was being chased. The one downfall with that town is that they don't like outsiders and that is what we were." Opening his eyes, he faces Tammy. "For the ten years that we lived there, we moved four times in town."

"Were your brother and sister bullied?" Tammy makes a note.

"They were, but not as bad as me," Charles looks down to the floor.

"How do you know that?"

"They weren't separated from the class like I was. I was put in special education in grade three and told that I had a reading problem. The funny thing was that by grade five, I was reading at a university level. So you tell me, who had the problem?" Charles makes eye contact.

"I guess I would say the school system."

"The way I saw it, was that they moved me out into another class because I was too smart. The only downside was that I was a sitting target for the bullies." Charles turns back to the window.

"I said it before: kids are cruel. If they were animals, they would have killed you." Tammy looks at Charles, sitting as if he was at peace.

"They tried; I just wouldn't die or give in. I was put in the hospital several times in those ten years. I was always missing school because I would take my books home and do the work at home. The teachers knew that was what I was doing, so they didn't mind. I should have just done homeschooling; I would have been better off. However, my marks did suffer in the long run. My average was in the high sixties when I was in Prussia." Charles closes his eyes. "My average in Sova for grade twelve was in the high nineties. It just goes to show what happens when you are not under stress what you can do. So can you see the picture, Tammy?"

"I can, Charles, and it doesn't look nice. How do you deal with having to live with that every day?"

"I don't think about it because when I do it makes me mad. I'll continue to paint the picture for you. When I was fifteen, I started to cook at a local restaurant and I was making my own money. Everyone asked me why I was doing a woman's job, so they labelled me again and called me a woman. In other words, I was making my own money and they didn't like it." Charles shakes his head from side to side in amazement. "As I said, my marks weren't the best because of what was happening to me. The teachers knew I was smart, but they turned a blind eye to the abuse. That was the help they gave me. They would see me getting beaten up and they would turn and walk away. I remember one day when I was being beaten by five other students. The teacher just stood there watching until it was over, and then had the nerve to ask me if I needed a hand getting back to my feet. I don't know, Tammy. Is that right?"

"That's not right in any book. I can't fathom why a teacher would stand there watching it and not doing anything to stop it. Do you forgive the teachers for what they did to you during those ten years?" Tammy was in disbelief over what Charles was saying.

"I do, Tammy. I do forgive them because they will get what's coming to them when they meet the man upstairs and my face will be the last thing they see before they die. The reason for that is because they will be asking for forgiveness." Charles takes a breath before continuing. "I think that I told you this already, but it was my sister who told our parents after seeing it for herself. The teachers changed some after my parents visited—not enough in my eyes, though."

"I know that this question is off topic, but do you have any other hobbies than writing? The reason I ask is because it helps me to draw a better picture of you." Tammy writes the word "hobbies," and underlines it.

"I do. Model trains, drawing, painting, and music. And I love to read, but I read slowly." Charles turns towards the window. "You didn't have to give me the reason for your question, because I knew why you asked. You are trying to find out what I did with my time for those ten years in Prussia. I found peace in art. Now with my art, I'm able to drift away into a different world, be it on paper or canvas, laying track, or making buildings for my train set, I'm at peace with myself. Like I have said, I'm writing a book, and the reason is because the story I'm telling will help people to get over their problems—or that's what I hope, anyway. All these sessions seem the same. I tell you about the things I've been through and you sit there and pretend to listen. That's the biggest problem with you counsellors, doctors, and such. You people just don't listen."

"Charles, I do listen. Why are you saying that I don't?"

"You tape each session that we have and when I'm talking you are off thinking of something different. I feel as though I'm talking to a machine or the wall. If you do listen, tell me why you record these sessions?"

"The reason is so I can play the session over again to see if I missed something."

"I'll tell you one thing—just turn the tape machine off and listen."

"Charles, I do listen to you, but I record all of the sessions with all of my patients." Tammy runs her finger down the file.

"So let it be then. Record this and continue to daydream. I thought you were different."

"Let's go back to talking about Prussia. How did you manage when you were at school?"

"You want to stay on that subject. I only wonder why? Like I have said, it was hard. I was alone all the time. And as I said before, I was taken out of regular class and put into what they called special ed. I had two different teachers, Jerry Smith from grade three to grade seven, and Donna Dillman until I moved to Sova." He takes another deep breath and opens his eyes before continuing. "During the breaks, I would stay in the classroom or the library. That's how I'd hide from the bullies—or tried to, anyway. The only downfall was that I had to go to my locker, which was in the hall, to get my books for class. To be honest, I often wished that I wasn't bullied. I only wonder what those ten years would have been like. I know that I'd probably be a different person today. I know that I've asked you this before, but I want to hear your answer again. Do you know what it's like to be bullied every day for ten years?"

"No I don't. I can't even imagine what it would be like. I can only see what you have drawn out for me. Charles, how do you feel about it now that you have been removed from it?"

"Ask yourself. How would you feel about it if you had to live it over and over in your mind and you think this is just a dream. The only downfall is that you are about to wake up and still be living in Prussia. Now you tell me, how would you feel?" Charles gets to his feet and walks over to the window.

"I think that you know how you feel and you are finding it hard to deal with it. If this is just a dream for you, don't wake up. Just stay asleep."

"You think that you know, but you don't. We've been talking a lot about Prussia for the last few sessions, and it's putting me back there. The memories are coming to life again. I had closed that door years ago and you have just opened it up. I'm feeling like I felt when we moved to Sova. I guess that I'm still upset and haunted about what had happened to me. It's like an open wound that won't heal over. The skin is trying to cover it, but it rips back open when I move. I think that is one of the reasons why I've done the things that I've done. You are here to help me, so help me." Charles walks back to the chair and sits back down.

"The best way I can help you is by talking about your past, and that is what we are doing. The more you let out how you feel about it, the more the wounds will heal. It's hard and you have been through a lot of pain. You're still traumatized from what has happened and now it's time to move on. It's going to hurt and the road is going to be long, but we are going down the right track."

"Tammy, do you know what the meaning of trauma is?" Charles makes eye contact.

"Yeah, it's a powerful shock that may have long-lasting effects." Tammy breaks eye contact.

"That's right. So now think about what you just said. The memories will always be there and I have to live with them every day and you don't." Charles looks at his watch. "I guess we will see you next week." Charles gets up and walks out of the office.

The morning goes quickly for Tammy and Carolin. At noon, they make their way to the restaurant. They walk in and get seated in a booth. "Did you read the article that I mentioned this morning?" Tammy unrolls the cutlery.

"I did. What I got from it was that it is passed on through the father. Everything else I already knew. What did you get from it?" Carolin turns to look outside.

"I guess I found out that it takes thousands of years for something like that to happen and that there will be more and more cases as time goes on. How did you know that it is a mutation?" Tammy asks this as the waiter comes with the menus.

"What else could mental illness be when you think about it? We try to understand the mind, and in doing so we have segregated the people with a mental illness because we can't explain what is happening to them. The one thing that is real is that this is only the beginning and there is no way to stop it." Carolin picks up the menu.

"As they say borderline genius, borderline insane." Tammy starts to look at the menu.

The waiter comes back to the booth. "Are you ladies ready to order?"

"I think so. Are you ready, Tammy?" Carolin hands back the menu to the waiter.

"I am. I'll have the blackened chicken salad." Tammy hands him the menu.

"And for you?" the waiter turns to Carolin.

"I'll have the clubhouse with a salad. Tammy, if you look at the facts about the mind, we will see that almost all of the geniuses that brought us everything we take for granted were a little bit insane at that time. Now look at what we have and I know that I've said this to you before."

"You probably have." Tammy pauses for a second. "There is something that I've been thinking about for the last few weeks. What if this life is just a dream?"

"You've been hanging around me too long because you're starting to think outside the box, which is good. In this world, we don't know what is real or not, and we have to make the choice to be able to learn who we truly are. Slowly, you're making that step and

I'll be here for you as you discover life from the spiritual side of the world. If this world is the dream, what are we going to learn together as friends, a community, and for ourselves?"

"Have you always thought that way, Carolin?" Tammy asks as their lunches are placed in front of them.

"No. I just knew that there was something out there besides the regular religions. The truth is out there and it's up to us to search it out. When was the last time you were at church?"

"I think about a month or so ago. Why do you ask?"

"I haven't been to church since I was living at home with Mom and Dad."

"Really? Should I go back then?"

"It's up to you. In a new age, you have respect for all faiths and belief systems."

"I see," Tammy says, and looks out the window.

Session Ten

It was two and Charles was sitting in the waiting room talking with Carolin. "So, are you single, Carolin?"

"Yes, I am and I don't date clients." Carolin looks over to him. "You can go in. Tammy is waiting for you."

Charles walks into Tammy's office and sits down in his chair. "It's a beautiful day today. The birds woke me up this morning at five. I guess getting up earlier is healthy, but they never put that in a night cook's schedule. How are you today, Tammy?"

"I'm doing well. And you?" Tammy opens his file.

"I'm alive and another day above ground is a good day." Charles makes eye contact with Tammy.

"How has your week been?" Tammy picks up her pen.

"It has been one that I wouldn't write home to mom about. I bumped into an old friend that I had in Sova when I was in high school. Spencer is his name and, well, we tied one on. He told me that he was just taking some time off from the oilrigs to see the country. Other than that, nothing really happened."

"Well, it's always nice to see old friends. What are we going to talk about today?"

"First things first, I wrote this poem last night. Do you want to read it?" Charles pulls out a folded sheet of paper from his pocket.

"Sure." Charles hands Tammy the paper and she starts to read it. "Charles, is your question about life or are you questioning the reason for your life?"

"Why don't you tell me? The meaning is in there. Or did you miss it, as you only skimmed it instead of reading it? Once again, you show that you're not paying attention."

"Charles, with this poem you ask God for help, and that is what is causing the questions in it. So you tell me, are you questioning life or just your own life?" Tammy hands back the poem.

"I'm questioning God and why He would let what happened to me in Prussia happen. Have you found God, Tammy?"

"I have and I follow His teachings, which have been placed in his book every day. Have you found God, Charles?" Tammy writes the word "God" in the file.

"I was turned away from my religion when I needed it the most." Charles turns toward the window.

"Well, let's talk about that starting from the beginning. How does that sound?" Tammy circles the word "God."

"Why not? First is the meaning of religion. A belief in, or a worship of, a higher power to be divine or having control of human destiny? In common terms, to believe that there is some-thing up there? So I'll start now, I was baptized as a Christian at the age of two months in the local church. Mom took us kids to church every Sunday, and Dad would come when he wasn't working. I thought that it was something that would help me as I grew up. When we moved to Sova, we kept going to church, and that is when I started to ask God why He was letting the bad things happen to me." Charles sighs before continuing. "During that time, God was dead to me because He wasn't stopping it. I thought that maybe I upset Him, and it was His way of punishing me. I started to resent going to church."

"How do you feel about it now that time in your life is over?"

"I still feel the same. When we left Prussia for Sova, I knew that life was getting better. I could feel the calming sensation when I would say the town's name. It was to me like God was saying to me that I going to be fine, and that He was sorry. The Sova year went by quickly, and then I was in Cunnings. I stopped going to church when I moved to Cunnings because I was doing other things and I was always working on Sunday morning at the hotel. Then a year passed and my life took a huge downturn. I went to the church that was near where I was living to ask for help to get my life back on track. The minister told me that because I wasn't a member there, they didn't have time for me. I took that as a slap in the face, and since then have been following the Pagan belief system because it has welcomed me with open arms." Charles leans back in the chair.

"Charles, the church is run by man. It wasn't God slapping you in the face, it was a minister who didn't want to help you. Why did you choose a belief like Pagan?" Tammy writes down the word "Pagan," and circles it.

"The reason is because it is the root to all the religions and belief systems today. There are other names, too, from the occult to New Age. I first experienced it when I was sixteen because my aunt follows its teachings. When I was in Cunnings and that minister did that to me, I called my aunt the next day and we talked for hours. She told me that God or the higher power has a plan for everyone. For the next few months, I would call her and she would help me learn how to deal with my past. It worked, and I have been making progress in understanding why I'm here. As I sit here today, I look at religions as nothing but cults." Charles laughs.

"Why do you say that?"

"That's all they are. The people that go to a building to pray are nothing but sheep following a flock that's led by an individual who reads from a book. With New Age, there is no written text to follow; what you follow is your spirit. Everywhere you go there is an energy that guides you there. In a way, you and I are meant to meet and learn something from one another. Until we learn what that is, we will continue having these sessions."

"Well, Charles, since you feel that we are here to learn, then you must learn how to function outside of that world and be a member of this world. Now I want to go back to when the minister turned you away. How did you feel about that?"

"How did it make me feel? It made me feel alone in the world and I was upset as well that he didn't care to help me. I was always told that God was there to help at any time. That night, I guess He didn't want to, and that is why I found a new way that the higher power would always be beside me." Charles looks at his watch. "It's almost that time again, Tammy. Are you going to tell me how to find what it is what I'm looking for?"

"I could say that it is in religion, but I don't want to stop you from finding it on your own. It's one of those things that as a person we have to find on our own and to try to lead someone to it is something that I can't do." Tammy closes his file.

"In the light of it, you're learning and it's good to see." Charles gets up from the chair. "See you next Monday, Tammy." he turns and walks out of the office.

Four-thirty comes to pass and the last client of the day leaves Tammy's office. A few minutes later, Tammy walks out with the file in her hands. "Carolin, here is the last file for the day. Do you think what we do helps people or are we just guiding them to a better life?"

"I think we do help, but I don't know for sure. Why do you ask?" Carolin gets up from her chair to put the file away.

"Just wondering. I'm on my way upstairs to see Tim. Can you lock up when you leave?"

"I can do that. Have a good meeting." Carolin sits back at her desk. "See you later. I'll give you a call tomorrow in the afternoon and we will go for a coffee."

"Sounds good." Tammy leaves the office for the elevators. After getting to Tim's office, she has a seat in the waiting room. A few minutes go by before Tim comes out.

"You're early. Come on in, Tammy." Tim makes eye contact with her.

Tammy gets up and follows Tim into his office. "How are you today, Tim?"

"It has been a good day. And how are you Tammy?" Tim sits down.

"Well, the truth is, the talk that we had yesterday helped and I'm feeling better about the situation between Matt and me." Tammy looks at the dreamcatcher.

"That's good. Did you talk to him or did you write a letter to him?" Tim opens up her file.

"We talked some this morning because I fell asleep before he got home last night. Where did you get that?" Tammy points at the dreamcatcher.

"I make them and I sell them to New Age stores in the area here. Would you like one?" Tim smiles.

"That's OK. I was just admiring how beautiful it was. Who taught you how to do that?"

"My grandfather taught me when I was about ten and I have been doing them since. I'll give you this one and you should hang it over your bed." Tim gets up and takes down the dreamcatcher. "This will bring pleasant dreams to you and Matthew."

"Thank you for this. You used Matt's full name, that's different. I only use his full name when we are fighting," Tammy holds the dream catcher up to her nose.

"I see. One thing my grandfather always said to me was to get someone's attention you should call them by their full name. It still works to this day. Anyway I feel the more you try to change him the more you will get mad. I'm sure other people have told you this before. By trying to change him, it puts stress on the relationship and that's not healthy for anyone. You need him to know that he is loved by you and that you would do anything to make the relationship work, but don't change yourself. He loves you for who you are and it probably frustrates him when you both fight. So with that being said, do you see what I mean?" Tim brings his hand up to his face. He then opens his hand, "The problem lies where you can't see past your own hand. By moving your hand down or to either side it opens up your vision to be able to see past. Remember that," he lowers his hand.

"I think I get what you mean. By me trying to change him I'm blocking the true him."

"That's right. The solution is let him be him and life, as strange as it can be, will happen. If down the road you break up, hey, that's life. Try to be you and let him be him. OK, that is all the time we have and if you need someone to talk to, talk to Matt because that is what he is there for." Tim closes the file. "Tammy, I'll be here if you need me as well, so good luck on your path that you take."

"Thank you, Tim." Tammy gets up and walks out of his office. As she walks home, she feels more confident and happy with what was happening in her life. At home, she makes herself something to eat before turning on the news.

At seven in the evening, Tammy leaves her house for a walk and a coffee at Mark's on the waterfront. At Mark's, she sits outside on the patio and listens to the city's sounds. She watches the ships and boats move around in the harbour as she sits in peace enjoying her coffee. Deep down she wishes that Matt was there with her to keep her company but he is at work. As she finishes her coffee, she gets up and leaves Mark's. She makes her way down the waterfront and walks up South Street to the hotel that Matt works at. She walks into the pub to see Matt standing at the bar in his whites. "Hi Matt," she walks up to him.

"Tammy, how are you babe?" Matt puts his arm around her.

"I thought that I would come to say hi," Tammy smiles at him.

"I'll see you later tonight Tammy, got to finish this one banquet and then I'll be home," Matt kisses her on the cheek.

"Yeah, maybe I'll stay here and have a couple of glasses of wine while I wait for you to get off," Tammy sits on the bar stool that is beside her.

"That sounds fine," Matt gets the bartenders attention. "Scott, put my girlfriend on my tab and bring her the wine list."

"No problem Matt."

"I'll see you in a bit Tammy," Matt walks back to the kitchen.

"So what will it be?" Scott asks as Tammy looks at the wine list.

"Scott, I'll have a red wine with a rich flavour. So give me that and the name is Tammy," Tammy flicks her hair out of her eyes.

"So a red it is. This is my personal favourite, I think you will like it Tammy," Scott shows her the bottle.

"Well, I'll try it and give you my opinion," Tammy smells the cork. Scott pours Tammy a glass of wine and gives it to her. She holds the glass up to her nose and inhales the aroma of the wine, and takes a sip she says, "Not bad, to be honest. It's very good."

"So you like it Tammy, that's good. Do you want me to leave the bottle with you?" Scott sets the bottle in front of Tammy.

"Sure," Tammy takes another sip of the wine.

"So what do you do for a living?"

"I help people deal with their lives."

"How long have you been doing that for?"

"About three years. How long have you been a bartender?" Tammy running her finger over the rim of the wine glass.

"I started here about a year ago as a part time job to help me pay for school."

"What are you taking in school?"

"I'm taking Business Administration and my major is finance. I have another two years until I'm finished, so I'll probably stay working here," Scott rips a bill off the order printer for a drink.

"What do you hope to gain from your degree?" Tammy looks at the hard liquor on the shelf.

"Hopefully a job with an accounting firm or with a big company," Scott sets the drink order on the side of the bar.

"That's sounds like a good goal, but what is your dream?"

"I guess my dream would be to settle down, get married and raise a family. You know, Matt never speaks of you here at work, much less anything personal. He is always about work and he doesn't really smile much either, other than when he is finished his shift. Is he like that outside of work?" Scott asks as another bill prints up.

"No, he keeps his personal life and work life separate. He doesn't talk about his job all that much at home other than when he has a real bad day," Tammy takes a sip of her wine.

"Sorry to ask. I just was wondering because all I get out of him when he is having a drink after work is sports and music. I knew that he wasn't single. So how long have the two of you been together?"

"We have known each other for three years and been dating for about the same amount of time. Now the question to you, are you single?" Tammy puts her empty glass down and fills it back up.

"I am. For right now it's the best situation for me. School and work keeps me certainly busy. When I'm done school I will look for someone then," Scott sets another order down on the bar.

"Be careful, because love happens to you when you are busy making other plans. It's something like life, it just happens," Tammy smiles.

"Thanks for the warning. I'll keep my radar on the lookout for love."

"Trust me, you will wake up one morning with a wedding ring on, children and you will not know how it all happened. That would be called life and you will think back to this conversation with me."

"How do you know that will happen?" Scott hears the printer going off again.

"I see it every day. Life moves at one speed and it's hard for most people to keep up because time flies. Some people are lucky and don't end up in hospital and others when they wake up it's a hospital room they see because they have had a mental breakdown. So mark my words," Tammy brings the glass of wine up to her lips.

"Well, if that's how it's going to be, I'll book an appointment with you now," Scott laughs.

"You're more than welcome to do so. I would love to pick your life apart and start you on the positive road to rehab," Tammy grins.

"You're kidding, right?" Scott sets the last drink order on the side of the bar.

"You are what, twenty? When I was your age I was at University taking my psychology degree. I have been out of school for a few years now and practicing for three years at my own practice. So I'm not joking. You pick the day and we will fit you in," Tammy picks up the bottle of wine and her glass. "I'm going to sit over in that booth so I don't take you away from your work."

About an hour passes before Matt comes out into the bar in his street clothes and sits down in the booth. "Well that's another day over. You ready to go home?" he smiles.

"Let's go," Tammy finishes off the bottle of wine.

Tammy and Matt walk out of the bar and out of the hotel onto the street. As they walk down the street together, Matt is on the side closest to the road. They hold hands all the way home and not a word is spoken between them the whole way. After crossing at the crosswalk, they arrive at home. Tammy unlocks the door and walks into the condo. Matt follows and closes the door, locking it behind him. They take off their shoes and embrace each other as if it was the first time.

It's Saturday morning and Matt's alarm clock is ringing. He slowly turns and shuts it off. Tammy rolls over and goes back to sleep. Matt gets out of bed and makes his way to the bathroom to get ready for work. He steps out of the washroom and heads for the kitchen to make a pot of coffee. As the coffee brews, he gets dressed for work. "Tammy, it's seven. Time to rise and shine," he nudges her.

 "Let me sleep," Tammy in a tired voice covers her head with a pillow.

 Matt grabs the pillow and pulls the covers off the bed. "Get up, I'll make you some breakfast before I go to work," he passes Tammy her housecoat.

 "Fine but after breakfast I'm going back to sleep," Tammy sits up on the bed and puts on her housecoat.

 Matt walks out of the bedroom and to the kitchen to make Tammy and him breakfast. He finds the frying pan and places it on the stove. He then opens the fridge door to get a few eggs. "Do you want French Toast or Fried eggs?" he asks as Tammy walks into the kitchen.

"French Toast sounds good," Tammy pours herself a coffee. "Nothing like a black coffee in the morning," she holds the coffee cup up to her nose.

"Want to pass me the bread sweetheart?" Matt cracks the eggs into a bowl and whips them up with a fork.

"Here you go," Tammy passes him the bread.

Matt checks the frying pan to see if it's hot enough. He dips the bread into the egg and puts two slices into the pan. A couple minutes passes before he flips them with a tong. "These first two are for you," he reaches for a plate. Another couple of minutes pass and then he uses his tongs to take the toast out of the pan. He then passes the plate to Tammy.

"Thank you," Tammy walks over to the table and sits down. "I forgot to get a fork."

"I'll bring you one and the syrup," Matt flips his toast out of the pan and onto his plate. He opens a drawer and gets two forks. He grabs the syrup from the counter and makes his way to the table handing Tammy a fork.

"Thanks. Do you know how long it has been since we sat down together for breakfast?" Tammy takes the syrup from Matt and pours it all over her toast.

"It's been some time. How long has it been since we ate anything together here at the condo?" Matt cuts up his toast with the fork.

"Maybe we could make this something we do on Saturday mornings. That way we could talk about how things are going with each other. It could be our quality time together. What do you think?" Tammy starts to cut her toast.

"If you think that it would be helpful then sure," Matt takes a bite of his toast.

"What did you want to talk about this morning when you woke me up?" Tammy dips her toast in the syrup on her plate.

"I think that it's time to move to a different part of the city," Matt gets up from the table to get himself more coffee.

"Why do you want to move to a different part of the city? Everything is in walking distance here and all of our friends live in this area," Tammy starts to eat her second piece of toast.

"You want to have kids, right?" Matt sits back down at the table.

"Yeah, what does moving have to do with it?" Tammy takes a sip of coffee.

"This is a three bedroom condo and its downtown. When we have kids, wouldn't you like a yard for them to play in? Just thinking about the future," Matt cuts up the rest of his toast.

"I knew that was what you were going to say. What would be wrong with living downtown?" Tammy asks and finishes her toast and coffee.

"Traffic for one thing, secondly we could get a bigger place in another part of the city after selling this place," Matt looks at his watch.

"Sell? I didn't buy this place, dad did. I give dad so much a month until it's paid off. So selling is out of the question."

"Your dad bought this place. When were you going to tell me that, Tammy?" Shaking his head, he continues. "Anyway, I got to get to work. I'll see you around nine or ten. I have 1,500 people to feed tonight." Matt picks the plates up from the table, goes into the kitchen with them, and places them in the sink. He fills his to-go mug with coffee and makes his way to the front door. Sitting down on the step, he puts his boots.

As Matt is about to leave, Tammy walks to the staircase. "I was going to tell you that Dad bought this place, but we—I mean, I— just kept forgetting to tell you."

"Well, it's just something that you should have in the beginning of the relationship. You could have said, 'Matt, I don't own the condo.' But you didn't. I'll see you after work." Matt walks out, slamming the door.

Tammy makes her way back to the bedroom and puts the blankets back on the bed. She lays back down and drifts off to sleep.

Session Eleven

It's two o'clock and Charles is sitting in the waiting room at Tammy's office. Tammy walks out and says, "Charles, you can come in." She motions for him to follow and turns around.

"I guess it's time for the help that I'm going to get today." Charles gets up from the chair and follows Tammy into the office. He sits down in the same chair as always.

"How was your week, Charles?" Tammy sits down and opens Charles's file.

"It has been good for the most part. I spent a good portion of it at work. I also had time to write some more poems." Charles makes himself comfortable.

"How is school going?" Tammy picks up a pen.

"I finished a week ago; I didn't realize that you would remember. I finished at the top of the class with an average of ninety-four. That's the reason why I worked so much last week." Charles turns to the window. "I can't remember if I told you that I'm looking for a new place to live or not, but I found one. I move in at the end of the month."

"I think that you said that. How are your roommates taking the news?" Tammy takes a sip of her water.

"The lease is up at the end of the month, so it doesn't matter what they think and, really, I don't care." Charles closes his eyes.

"I didn't know that it was that bad living with two women. So where in the city are you moving to?" Tammy writes down the word "moving" in his file.

"I'm moving down to Church Street. It's just two blocks from where I live right now. It will be nice to have my own space again. The peace and quiet, not having to wonder whose time of the month it is, and not hearing them fight. I'm so looking forward to this move." Charles opens his eyes.

"Did you know these girls before you moved in with them?"

"No, I was introduced to them by a friend. They needed a third roommate, so my friend mentioned it to me. I thought that it was a good idea at the time, but now I know that I made a mistake and the lesson I learned was that I'm better off living on my own." Charles turns back to make eye contact with Tammy. "So, what do you want to talk about today?"

"Well, I had a week to think about that. The question I have is, do you have a girlfriend down here in Metro?" Tammy writes "girlfriend" in the file.

"My love life, that's funny. I don't have one. I've been single since I was twenty-two, and it's better like that for me." Charles turns back to the window.

"Why do you say that?"

"I'm not looking for a relationship, because I have very little time to myself as it is. That's one reason; another is that I want to experience life before I settle down. There is another, and that is that I'm a nice guy who has a soft heart. You know that the nice guys always finish last." Charles starts cracking his knuckles.

"That's not true."

"It's true. Who do you want? The nice guy that treats you right and talks to you when there is a problem? Or the guy that doesn't respect you and fights with you at the drop of a hat—aka, 'the fixer upper.' The nice guy who cares? Or the guy who doesn't? So, Tammy, who do you want?" Charles glances at Tammy.

"I would want the nice guy."

"Most women say that, but when they get the nice guy, the relationship doesn't work because they're not used to the treatment. For this reason, nice guys are hard to find because they are always working, going to school, and pursuing their dreams. They also know that when the time is right, love will find them. Do you understand?" Charles lets out a sigh.

"I think that you have had a few bad relationships in your past. You said that you haven't had a girlfriend since you were twenty-two. So, tell me, how many girlfriends have you had?"

"I'll comment on the first thing you said and answer your question at the same time. I was in two good relationships. The first relationship was with Kathie. That lasted for two years before she moved. The other one was with Nicole, and it lasted for two years, as well. We broke up because I changed my life by moving back to Sova."

"Can you tell me more about your relationships with women as you were growing up?" Tammy writes more notes.

"So you want to know the story. I guess I'll tell you then. Growing up in Prussia, I never had girls around me because I wasn't one of the cool people. I know that you know that. In Sova, I never tried to get to know the girls there because I wasn't comfortable around them, but I would talk to them. Not like in Prussia. When I moved up to Cunnings to go to college, a couple of friends introduced me to Kathie. She looked at me with the eyes of an angel and told me not to be afraid. I walked over to her and she put out her hand. I took her hand and kissed the top of it." Charles sneezes and continues. "If it would have come out any harder, my eyes would have popped out of my head. Anyway, when we met, I don't know if the stars were just right or what, but we fell for each other.

"The real first date was fun, it happened about a month after we met. On that night, I went over to her apartment to pick her up. She said that she had to go to her parents' for a minute and then we would be off. I had my ideas, but she had others. We went over to her parents' and she said that I should come in with her. Her plan was for me to meet her parents, and this was the night I got introduced to the crime world. Anyway, her dad had a million questions for me to answer during supper. Her dad is Sir, and I know that I have mentioned him before. So that was our first date in a nutshell.

"Kathie was studying at the U of C for her law degree. For the first few months, it was hard for us to find time together, but we made it work. After she finished her second year, she got accepted into Brown University of Law in York. It's about a twenty-four hour drive from here. She wanted me to move with her, but I didn't. We broke up on good terms. I explained to her that I wanted to stay in Cunnings to finish my cooking papers. She cried, and I did, as well. Looking back on it now, if I had moved with her, I would be married and probably we would have kids."

"Did you two ever fight?"

"No. We always talked about our feelings and why we felt the way we did. When there were problems, and we did have them, we would sit over a coffee and talk about it. As I said, it was a good relationship that lasted two years." Charles glances at Tammy again before looking out the window.

"You two never had a fight? I find that hard to believe."

"Like I told you, if you talk, there shouldn't be a fight. One of the biggest things that we did was not try to change each other. That made for less friction between us." Charles closes his eyes.

"Was it the same with Nicole?" Tammy shakes her head in disbelief.

"It was. She is Kathie's best friend, so we knew each other for some time before going out. The only difference was that I moved. Nicole wanted to come with me but I told her that I needed to change my life," Charles opens his eyes.

"Those breakups must have been hard on you." Tammy continues writing down notes.

"Not at all. I'm not like other guys. I move on with my life. To ask a question, do I think about them? I do, but I have grown and changed since that time of my life. I'll always walk the hard road because you learn more that way. As well, I'll always lie in the bed I've made for myself. The reason I say that is because it's my life to live; no one else can live it for me." Charles turns and makes eye contact.

"You know, Charles, what you just said is selfish." Tammy glares at him.

"Call it what you will, but I call it knowing who I am. I think that I'll tell you about the friends who introduced me to Kathie.

Their names are Logan and Jay, and they are both four years older than me. I met them at a bar on White Ave., which is one of the bar streets in Cunnings. They were trying to be drug dealers and it wasn't their calling. I walked into Club X; this is where I met them, at around midnight for something different from the pubs that I had been going to. The day I think was September the fifth. I have mentioned them in an earlier session, but here is the true story. What I told you before is true; I just left out some details.

"I walked up to the bar and this big black man was standing in front of me. So I thought to start a conversation with him when he turned around. He told me that his name was Logan, and that he was from New Amsterdam. He then asked me if I wanted to buy some weed. I said no and that I would buy him a drink. After getting him the drink, we continued talking about things. He told me that he was an investment banker for a major bank. Logan then introduced me to Jay, who was his partner in crime. Jay worked in one of the hospitals in the city as a druggist. The one thing they didn't know was that I would change them forever." Charles leans back in the chair.

"How would you change their lives?"

"I'll tell you. On the night when I met Kathie's father, Sir, we sat and talked after the meal in his study. He asked me if I wanted to make some extra money. I replied, yes, not knowing what I was going to get into. Sir then asked if I wanted to go for a drive. So we left the house and drove to the west end of the city. As we drove, he filled me in on what I would be doing, and that was delivering large amounts of drugs to the suppliers who supplied the street dealers. Sounds simple, but it wasn't.

"We arrived at a warehouse a couple of minutes later. He told me that he would have to get me into the system, and that I would be given a route. He told me that I would need a couple of people that I trusted to help me. That is when I changed Logan and Jay. That night, I called them both and asked if they wanted to make some easy money. Both of them said yes, so the three of us were put into the system and given a route. The route we got was in the central core of the city, where there was a lot of violence among the four main gangs in the city. Best way to put it is to say a turf war was happening at that time." Charles looks at his watch.

"I see, let's change topics for a moment. When you were in Prussia, were there any girls that you liked?"

"There was. Her name is Kelly Ehrman. She was in the same grade as me." Charles closes his eyes. "She knew that I liked her. She always hung around the guys who were into sports. I remember this one time in grade eleven, she needed a short story written for her English class. She came to me and asked if I would write it for her. She knew that the teacher wouldn't know that I wrote it because I wasn't in Mr. Downs's English class."

"Did you write it?" Tammy writes a note about him being used.

"I did. I thought that if I did something nice for her, she would want to hang around me, but I was dead wrong. She said thanks, rewrote it into her handwriting, and handed it in as her own." Charles opens his eyes.

"She used you, which must have hurt. Did you tell her teacher?"

"No, I didn't want for her to get in trouble. It didn't matter anyway, because a few months later, we left that town." Charles shakes his head from side to side slowly.

"Charles did you tell your parents about these things?" Tammy sets down her pen.

"No, and why would they care that their son wasn't an athlete? I didn't even tell them what was happening to me in Cunnings. Tammy, it's that time again. I'll see you next week," Charles gets up from the chair and walks out of the office.

It's two o'clock in the afternoon when the phone rings and Tammy answers it. "Hello."

"Tammy, it's Carolin. You want to go for that coffee that I mentioned yesterday?"

"Sure. I'll meet you at Mark's in ten minutes." Tammy hangs up the phone. She walks down the stairs to the door and put on her shoes. As she walks down the street to Mark's, she thinks about her appointment with Charles that was happening on Wednesday morning. How it was going to go and what he was coming back for? All the questions that you could imagine run through her head. The one that sticks out the most is if he had changed or not. When she gets to Mark's, she opens the door and walks in to see Carolin waiting in line. "Carolin," Tammy says, trying to get her attention.

Carolin turns and sees Tammy standing in the back of the line. "Tammy, I'll get your coffee. Find us a seat." Carolin waves to Tammy.

Tammy makes her way onto the patio and finds a seat under an umbrella. A few minutes go by before Carolin comes out with the coffees. "Thank you. I will get it next time." Tammy takes one of the coffees from Carolin.

"So how are things going today?" Carolin sits down.

"Not too bad. Told Matt that the house was bought by dad." Tammy picks up her coffee and takes a drink.

"What sparked that conversation?"

"Matt wants to move out of downtown."

"Why? Everything is in walking distance where you guys are at." Carolin makes eye contact.

"Well, he wants us in a house with a yard and such. The reasoning is because he doesn't want our kids to grow up in downtown." Tammy looks away.

"I don't see his point. The only difference is that there will be more work during the summer and winter. You guys only have one car, so how will that work? Is one of you going to take the bus?" Carolin turns her head to look out on the water of the harbour which, for some reason, is like a mirror.

"I know I didn't want to start a fight this morning. I'm almost sure that Matt is mad at me for not telling him from the start that

Dad owns the condo." Tammy sees one of her patients walking on the boardwalk.

"I would be, so don't be surprised if that is the topic when he gets off work tonight."

"Yeah, I feel that there will be a fight when he comes home from work, but I could be wrong." Tammy looks down at her coffee.

"At least you told him that your dad owns the condo. Let's not focus on what could be happening tonight because it will only make the day seem longer than it is. Let's talk about the fact that we are able to do what we want, and when we want to do it." Carolin smiles.

"You know, you're crazy," Tammy laughs. "As I was coming down here, I was thinking about Charles's return to counselling after he left three years ago. I think that he is going to be telling the same story that he told me last time. The reason I think that is because that is where he is hiding. Experiencing what he did made him build a wall between himself and the rest of the world. It's the poor-me attitude that he's lived with for the majority of his life, and it hinders his ability to make new friends because he will always tell that story."

"You could be right, or maybe he has stopped that 'poor me,' and is starting to try to make friends in a new way. I wasn't the one seeing him during those sessions, it was you, so to predetermine by what has happened in the last three years is not right." Carolin takes a sip of her coffee.

"I'm not predetermining anything by what has happened in those three years. I'm just saying that I don't think that he has changed." Tammy looks to the harbour.

"That is predetermination by saying that he probably hasn't changed. You can say what you think, but you are putting him in a box and labelling it. And when he is here, you are going to treat that label. Am I right?"

"You got me there." Tammy turns her attention back to face Carolin.

Carolin and Tammy continue to talk as they drink their coffee.

Session Twelve

Charles is sitting in the waiting room with a binder of his writing. Checking his watch, he sees it is ten to two. "Carolin, is Tammy waiting for me or does she have someone in with her?"

"No, but she is on the phone. She should be done shortly." Carolin gets up, walks over to the coffeemaker, and pours herself a coffee.

About five minutes pass before Tammy comes out of her office holding some papers. She hands them to Carolin. "OK, Charles. Come on in." she walks back into her office.

Charles follows. As he gets into the office, he sits down in the same chair as last time. "I brought you some of my writing to read. There are about 200 pages of essays and poems. I hope you have a chance to read some of them." He sets the binder on Tammy's desk.

"So, how has your week been, Charles?" Tammy opens his file.

"It has been good. I got a lot done on my book that I'm writing. The title of it is going to be 'Angel.' The basis of the book is a man who, after changing his life, finds himself alone in the world. I got the idea after our last session. Work is, well, work. It has its good days and bad days. I got a few calls, one from my friend Jen and another from my parents." Charles turns to look out the window.

"That's good, and I'll read some of your work throughout the week. Let's get started. What would you like to talk about today?"

"I don't know, why don't you choose a topic and I'll go from there." Charles closes his eyes.

"Do you have any dreams that you would like to reach?" Tammy writes down the word "dreams."

"I have lots of dreams. One is to be a published author, another is to own my own restaurant." Charles opens his eyes to see a bluebird fly past the window. "Do you have any dreams, Tammy?"

"I do."

"That's good. Now go for them and don't stop until you have reached them. My mom once said to me to dream big and go for them. The reason she said that was because so many people have big dreams but never go for them. To get to your dreams, you make goals that are on the same path as your dream. As you obtain your goals, your dream is that much closer." Charles turns and makes eye contact with Tammy.

"That's a positive way of looking at how to reach your dreams. My father always told me to keep your goals in reach and your dreams just out of your reach, so that way you'll still follow them—another way you can look at it, if you want." Tammy breaks eye contact.

"One of my biggest dreams was to move back down here and I know that I told you that before, so in a way I'm living my dreams already. The rest are going to fall into my lap as I strive forward toward them. There have been many people who have tried to stop me from reaching my dreams and goals, and I have left them on the road dead, metaphorically speaking." Charles looks back out the window.

"Charles, how has the relationship with your other family members changed over time?"

"From dreams to family relations—that's some spin in a different direction. I'll tell you one. My cousin, Tim, and I are three months apart in age. When we were little, we saw each other every summer in the mountains where he lived. We would go down to the river and throw rocks and talk about the things that we wanted to be when we grew up. He wanted to be a photographer and I wanted to be a doctor. Anyway, he is a heavy-duty mechanic and I'm a cook—so much for him and I going after those careers. The dreams that we have when we are kids are pushed aside when we get older. Too bad we can't think like that when we get older; if we do, we are told to grow up. Tim is now married and has a son. That's further than I have ever got in my life. Now the relationship with him is so distanced that I wouldn't even know what to say if I called him. That's the same for the rest of my cousins," Charles sighs.

"I understand. As we get older, we change sometimes for the better. The pain in changing is that time takes its toll on us and we often find ourselves wondering what happened." Tammy takes a sip of her water.

"What did I tell you about that understanding thing? You'll never understand what I've been through. You have never walked in my shoes. You don't know what it is like to live every day with the hope that it isn't a dream."

"I haven't walked in your shoes, but the pain that you have been through has shaped you to this point. You're positive with a negative outlook on life. You talk about dreams but you have forgotten to live for them. Your past was hard for you; you have to make peace with it and let it go. That's why you need to open up and put down your guard for me so I can help you."

"How do you heal someone's mental scars? How do you make peace with the past when it keeps you up every night? Tell me that! You tell me that! My dreams are the only things that keep me going. If I didn't have them, I wouldn't want to continue living and going into my relationships with my family, other than my parents, they wouldn't care if I was alive or dead."

"I don't think that's true. You may think that, but your family will always be there for you."

"You just don't get it! I'm the black sheep of the family!" Charles slams his hand on the chair's armrest. "You know, life happens. It's up to us to figure out how to live it. Time doesn't stop, we do." Charles looks at his watch, "It's that time of day, and I'll see you next week." He gets up and leaves the office after only fifteen minutes.

"Tammy? Are you OK?" Carolin asks, setting down her empty coffee cup.

"I was just remembering something. Sorry about that." Tammy gives her head a shake.

"There is something on your mind, and it's not your relationship with Matt. So come clean, what's on your mind?" Carolin makes eye contact.

"It's Charles. I have been remembering bits and pieces of the sessions we had. I've been seeing his face every time I close my eyes. The look in his eyes that he had in every session was the same; it was like he wasn't even there inside. The look was dark, black almost. I think that he was telling the horror story that was his life. I really didn't make any progress with him until the thirteenth session. He gave me some of his writing and the picture I got was that he was alone all his life and his writing was the world he knew. I just couldn't imagine that someone that smart being alone. It just couldn't happen in today's world." Tammy looks away.

"Tammy, smart people are always alone because only in solitude they find peace with themselves and the world. Talking to the common person is hard for them. They have very few friends and the friends that they have are the misfits of our society and that's where the smart people fall. It's sad to say, but that's how this world works. Our civilization thinks inside a box and those people think outside the box. When they get put down for so many years because of it, they disconnect themselves from society. Most of them go insane and end up in the mental wards of hospitals. Have you forgotten what your father always told us when we were growing up?"

"Yeah, borderline genius, borderline insane. He also said that to have a mental illness, you have to be intelligent. So what you are saying is that we alienate the smart ones to the misfit side of things and life happens to the rest of us as they wait for their time to be part of it all. That's bull—where did you get that information?"

"You remember about two years ago when I was doing night classes at the university for sociology? One of the topics was on how we as a whole treat the intelligent with ignorance. That's why those people live a life that no one else could ever obtain. They keep their life simple, and at work they rise through the ranks very quickly. The only downfall for them is that they have no social skills. They are the ones who run our companies, hospitals, military, and so on. The reason is because they are focused on one thing, and that's to achieve their goals and dreams. Most of them think in a systematic way and that's why they get what they want." Carolin leans back.

"You got that all from that class? Maybe I should have taken it, too." Tammy gets out of the chair. "I need another coffee. Do you want another?"

"Sure." Carolin hands Tammy her coffee cup.

Tammy walks into Mark's and goes up to the counter to ask for another two cups of coffee. She walks out back to where they are sitting and asks, "What makes us do the thing we do?"

"It really depends on what you mean, but it's mostly caused by need. We need something, so we go get it." Carolin takes the coffee.

"I think you misunderstood what I meant. What I meant was why do people act the way they do?" Tammy sits down.

"There are many reasons why people do what they do. Why does a bully do what they do? The answer lies with what is happening at home and in their past. So, to answer your question, it lies with what is going on in their lives. The thing that I think that you are trying to find out is whether Charles has lived his life alienated for the most part."

"How do you know?"

"You can just tell. People who are by themselves all the time walk differently, talk differently, and, when they talk, they are very well spoken. What else can I say?"

Tammy and Carolin continue to talk about the little things in life. Even though Charles is on Tammy's mind, she doesn't speak his name again during the coffee. At around four o'clock, they leave Mark's and part ways.

Tammy walks along the harbour alone with her thoughts. She sees the boats and ships in the water going about their business. As she looks up the hill, she sees the skyline of Metro being shadowed by Citadel Hill. She turns to go up Spring Garden Road until she hit South Street. Turning left on South, she starts to walk to Point Pleasant Park.

With the slight breeze, Tammy gets a chill as she walks. Her thoughts are spinning nonstop about Wednesday's appointment with Charles. How has he changed? Why is he coming back? Was this his choice? These are just a few of the questions going through her head, but the biggest one is what if Charles is the man that her dad had mentioned just six days earlier? What would she do if that were the case? She doesn't know what to think. As she gets closer to the park, she tries to clear her mind of all thoughts.

Tammy finally gets to the park after the ten-minute walk, and enters the trail that runs through it. She makes her way down to Old Fort Basil, near the mouth of the harbour. Looking back, all she can see are the trees, the paths of the park, and other people walking along them. She sits down on the grass and leans against one of the large rocks near the old fort. Closing her eyes, she listens to the waves crashing against the seawall. At last, her mind is clear and she has found that peace that she has always been looking for.

Tammy opens her eyes after about an hour to see a sailboat going by the park. Getting to her feet, she starts to walk home, about a fifteen-minute walk down South Street to Morris. When she gets to her door, she unlocks it and walks in. After taking off her shoes, she makes her way to the kitchen to put a pot of water on for pasta. She puts on a pot of coffee, as well.

She walks into the living room and turns on the TV to the news channel and sits down in her chair. The news of the day is about a terrorist attack on a subway in Londinium. She turns off the TV, shaking her head at what kind of world they're living in. *This war on terror is a threat to any First-World country and it had been going on since the towers in New Amsterdam were brought down some few years earlier by the same terrorist group. What is their problem with the rest of the world? Why do they have to kill the innocents to say that we are the ones that were to blame for all the world problems?* Tammy thinks.

Getting up from her chair, she walks back into the kitchen to make her pasta. She empties the box into the boiling water and turns down the pot to half heat. She gives the pasta a stir; turning around to the coffee pot, she pours herself a cup.

Tammy then hears a key rattle in the lock on the door. The door opens and Matt walks in after a long day at work. "Tammy, are you here?" Matt calls, as he closes the door.

Tammy walks over to the top of the steps. "I am. How was work?"

"Not bad. Chef let me off early tonight. I think this is the earliest I've ever been off on a Saturday. What did you do all day?" Matt sits down on the steps and takes off his boots.

"Not too much. Had coffee with Carolin and went for a walk. I just got home about a half hour or so ago." Tammy sits down on the top step.

"That's good. Have you eaten yet?" Matt makes his way up the stairs.

"No, but I'm cooking some pasta." Tammy gets up to her feet.

"Anyway, about the conversation we were having this morning. Why did your father buy this place?" Matt walks past Tammy and heads to the kitchen.

"Because I couldn't get the mortgage or I would have." Tammy walks to the kitchen.

"So, why didn't you get your dad to cosign?" Matt picks his coffee cup and fills it.

"Dad said that he would take out the mortgage and I pay him. That way, if I'm short one month, it won't affect my credit score." Tammy opens the fridge and pulls out the pasta sauce.

"Won't affect your credit? What other bills do you have? You don't have a car payment to make and your office rent comes out of your office account. All you have is a credit card and what you pay your father. I don't understand why you wouldn't be able to get a mortgage. You have a job that pays well above average, so why? Tell me." Matt picks up a fork and stirs the pasta.

"I was in my first year of university when I was going to buy this place and the bank said that I was a high risk because I was a student." Tammy gets a small pot off the shelf for the pasta sauce and places it on the stove.

"So when you finished school and started to work, you should have told your dad that you were going to take over the payments at the bank and to sign it over into your name. Did you think of that?"

"Why are you trying to make me look stupid?" Tammy asks, angrily.

"I'm not making you look stupid, it's just simple questions. If I had the money, I would buy this place off your dad because that way we could sell and find a new place in Clayton Park. Then we could get married and start a family." Matt says.

"Clayton Park? We couldn't afford that area of the city. Houses start at $500,000 and that is only for a three-bedroom." Tammy laughs, pouring the pasta sauce into the pot.

"And how much is this condo worth? We are downtown, there are three bedrooms and underground parking. So how much did your dad pay for this place?" Matt drains the pasta.

"About $750,000, after all the paper work."

"And you have been paying on it for about seven years, and for the past three years I have been giving you $600 a month. How much of that do you give your father?" Matt pulls a couple of plates out of the cabinet.

"I pay Dad $2,100 a month. I didn't start to pay him until I was done school and started working. The lease on the office is mine though." Tammy turns off the sauce.

"Let's say this: a thirty-year mortgage on a $500,000 house is about $1,400 a month. You seeing what I'm saying here?" Matt puts the pasta onto the plates.

"Matt, we're not moving. We are close to everything, including the hospital. All of our friends live down here and, well, look at the traveling time to work in the morning. You would drive to work and I would probably have to take the bus because we only have your car. So we would have to look at getting another car and the list goes on. Did you think of these things when you got the idea? But that is you. Think with your big head and not your little head. There are pros and cons and you got to look at both, which is another thing you forget to do." Tammy pours the sauce onto her pasta and passes it to Matt.

"What? Do you think I'm stupid now? I'll tell you one thing, I'm three years older than you and before you knew me, I was living a different life. Mommy and Daddy didn't do anything for me. All they did for me was keep a roof over my head until I turned eighteen. After I finished high school, they took me to York, and dropped me off at the dorms of the college I was going to be attending. Before they drove away, they said to me, 'Now Matt, have fun. If you need help, call.' I was a small-town kid in a city that I didn't know how to get around in. I came up from nothing to what I have today. What would you do if your parents did that to you?" Matt walks out of the kitchen and sits down at the table.

"You're going into that poor-me attitude. Matt, we come from two different worlds. I live in the present and you are living in the past. Let it go. You had a challenge thrown at you and you survived. You should be proud of that." Tammy sits down at the table.

"Poor me." Matt starts getting mad. "You are pulling your counselling crap on me. Stop and think about that for a second. When you have a bad day, who do you come see? Who hears about it all night? Me. When I have a bad day, I don't bring it home."

"No, you come home drunk. I don't think you want to go down this path that you are choosing."

"What path?"

"For the last year, I have had to listen to you and how your life has been so bad that you wish that you would just die. So don't give me that line."

"What?" Matt sputters.

"If you're going to act like a kid, I'll treat you like a kid who is having a temper tantrum! You need to relax!"

"Yeah, that's going to help." Matt gets up and slams his plate in the sink, breaking it on contact.

"I'm going over to my parents', so don't wait up." Tammy passes Matt and heads toward the door.

"I won't because I have to work at six in the morning, so don't wake me when you come home." Matt slams the bedroom door.

CHAPTER eight

It's five o'clock Sunday morning and Matt's alarm is going off. Getting up, Matt looks to see that Tammy is not in bed. Thinking nothing of it, he makes way to the bathroom to get ready for work. He then goes into the kitchen to pour himself a cup of cold, old coffee. Making his way to the living room, he sees Tammy sleeping on the sofa. Not wanting to wake her, he walks back to the kitchen, drinking his coffee. He sits down at the table and writes a note for Tammy, apologizing for the fight the night before. As he looks up he sees that it is a quarter to six, and he knows he must be on his way to work. He makes his way down the stairs and sits on the step to put his boots on. He walks out of the condo and closes the door quietly behind him.

Session Thirteen

Charles walks into Tammy's office and sits down in the chair. "Good afternoon, Tammy. How was lunch?"

"It was fine. Why do you ask?" Tammy opens up his file.

"The reason is I was watching you and Carolin eating at the restaurant as I was sitting on one of the park benches across the street. Where are we starting today?" Charles gets comfortable in the chair.

"Well, let's start with how your week went." Tammy picks up a pen.

"My week started with me running into my old roommates after our last session. They are not that happy with me, but I don't care. Had a meeting with my boss and he is quite pleased that I'm still coming here and getting things worked out. The strange thing is he still thinks that I'm nuts, so it makes for an interesting work-place. Had a long talk with my parents, and they asked me if I wanted to move back home. They think that me being down here away from them is what is causing me to come to see you. I told them not to worry, and that their baby was doing fine. As well, I did some writing." Charles looks out the window.

"Charles, I was able to read some of your writing. I have a question. Do you feel alone in the world?"

"I don't feel alone in the world. What gave you that impression?" Charles turns to her.

"Your writing does. What I get from it is pain and loneliness; almost like that you are hiding from people. I might have got the wrong meaning from them, so tell me." Tammy writes the word "denial" in the file.

"Some of those writing happened when I was stoned on pot, so I guess that there is a chance that could be the meaning of some of them. Let's move on from that subject." Charles smiles and turns back to the window.

"Charles, when you sleep, do you dream at night?" Tammy makes a note of his drug use.

"I do, and sometimes I have nightmares. Why do you ask?" Charles closes his eyes and leans back.

"Do you remember them?" Tammy takes a sip of her water.

"Sometimes, when I do, I write them down." Charles opens his eyes and looks down at the floor. "I've told you my dreams already.

I'm living the nightmare because I know when I wake up I'll be seventeen and in Prussia."

"That won't happen. This is not a dream."

"If this is not a dream, then tell me what it is?"

"This is real life. If it was a dream, would you be able to reach your highest goals and dreams?"

"Tammy, this is a dream that has been ongoing since I was seventeen. Moving out of Prussia was a dream and when I wake from this, I will be there or in heaven. That is the sad thing about it." Charles makes eye contact.

"Charles, what is your heaven?" Tammy writes down the word "heaven."

"My heaven is a house in the mountains near a lake, with fruit trees all over the site, and a big garden, and my soulmate with me. That's my heaven."

"I guess that Prussia would be hell for you, then."

"You got that right. It's amazing what happens when you listen." Charles breaks eye contact and continues. "I'll tell you about the dream I had last night. I was walking through a city that was void of life, no one around. There was piano music playing, but I didn't know where it was coming from. I wonder what it means."

"It might mean that you are feeling alone in the world." Tammy taps her pen on the file.

"Maybe, but it could mean that I'm empty inside and the city is me. I'm devoid of life and that is what the emptiness means."

"If you think that, it very well could be."

"Do you have another appointment after mine?"

"No, I don't. Monday is a short day for me. Why do you ask?"

"I was thinking that we could go for a coffee down at Midnight's, you know, get away from these walls and out into public."

"That is something that we can't do." Tammy looks away from Charles.

"I just want to show you where I do some of my writing and it's the coffee shop that my aunt and I go to."

"How often do you go for coffee with your aunt?"

"We normally go once a week after supper on Mondays. Do you know how hard it is for me being down here?"

"I don't. Why don't you tell me?"

"It's hell because I'm so far away from my family. I have family down here but it is not like having my parents here. As much as my parents get on my nerves, I do miss them. It was my idea to move down here, one of my dreams that came true. Now I'm lost. Sometimes, I wonder why I left everything that I knew to start over down here." His eyes on a picture on the wall, Charles continues. "I guess if you follow your dreams they will come true. This was my choice; no one else made it for me."

"My dad always said that if you follow what your heart is telling you, you will see the potential that you have in this life."

"You know, I have never followed my heart because every time that I have, I've been hurt in some way or another. The thing that stops me from losing my mind is the fact that I know that the creator, or God, has something planned for me."

"Have you ever thought about becoming a monk?" Tammy leans back in her chair.

"Where did that come from? You really didn't think about that question, because it is not related to what we are talking about. To answer that stupid question, no, I never thought about becoming a monk," Charles smirks and shakes his head.

"I was just thinking that when the church turned you away that maybe you would have found a new belief."

"I did study different faiths and found out that they all follow the same ideology except for one and that is the pagan belief. Its name is New Age now—it just sounds better, I guess. That is what I follow now, but with my own ideas. I'll tell you something, all religions brainwash their followers into believing this and that and the worshippers are nothing but mindless sheep that believe what they are being told. I follow what is the original belief and the truth. My aunt that I have coffee with has helped to expand my soul to the realization that I'm the God of War and Peace, the oldest soul, and the first soul that the creator, or God, created. Then there is you, a young soul trying to understand this world and that is why you are in psychology," Charles laughs.

"Do you wonder why your boss thinks you need help? I'm not judging by any means, but you think you are a god. And for the record, maybe I'm an older soul than you." Tammy writes down "god complex" in the file.

"It's in your eyes; they don't lie." Charles makes eye contact and continues. "You have your faith, but you are a scared child because that's what the establishment would have you believe. You haven't really lived, have you? You are on the line of hope that there is an afterlife. Get all that junk out of your head that the church has put there and come over to the real world. Then you will have control and you'll know who you are."

"Why are you judging me, Charles?" Tammy breaks eye contact.

"I'm not judging you. I don't have to. I'm only pointing out the flaws and giving you the truth. From the first day I walked in here, I knew that it wasn't me needing the help, it was you. The school teaches you the book method, or tells you to think inside a box, and then they tell you to help your clients to think inside that box. It's like a doctor saying that there is something wrong with your thinking because you don't fit into the box. I think that I have mentioned this before. Here is the question: have you got me figured out yet?" Charles puts his hands over his mouth.

"I do."

"Then tell me, Tammy: who am I?" Charles lowers his hands.

"You are a man with a troubled past. What happened to you in Prussia made you snap when you lived in Cunnings? That's the reason why you were in the drug world. But you never told me about the year that you lived in Sova before you moved to Cunnings. Were you bugged there, as well? Maybe you started to snap in Sova. After all, ten years of abuse would make anyone go insane. And all that time without friends, the loneliness by itself would make anyone with a sound mind fall. I'm surprised that you didn't kill anyone. So Charles, tell me: what happened during grade twelve?"

"You want to know? First off, you don't know who I am, but I'll tell you about grade twelve. Dad moved up to Sova in the first part of the spring. I moved up on the fifteenth of August. I got a job at a local restaurant when I got there. For about a month, we lived behind the hospital in a tent trailer. When school started, I went to class and got my timetable figured out. On a regular day, I would have three to five spares. I was welcome in the town, but during that year I didn't make any friends because I didn't know who I could trust. So I was alone, but I did have a nickname and it was Bubble Boy."

"I see. The only difference was that you didn't get bugged, but you were still alone. Charles, since you have moved down here to Metro, have you made any friends?"

"Not really. They are more of acquaintances than anything else. The only thing that is keeping me here is school but I'm done that now. I can find work anywhere, so my job is just money that is paying my rent and other bills." Charles glances over to the corner to the right of the window where there is a globe.

"So even where you are down here, you still are alone, except for the family you have down here. I now understand what your writing is about. It's the only real friend that you have in this world. As well, your dreams are those of a person who lives them by going after them."

"I'm just Charles Davis from Hillsdale, why would anyone want to be my friend?" Charles shakes his head slowly.

"So you would have someone to talk to that isn't family."

"That's why I keep coming back here. This is my coffee with the real world," Charles laughs.

"I think that all the time that you have spent alone has eaten you up inside. When you lived in Cunnings, did you feel alone?"

"Not really, because I was always around Logan, Jay, and the girls."

"If you hadn't been running drugs during that time, would those relationships have been there?" Tammy makes eye contact with Charles.

"I don't know. So what you are trying to say to me is if I wasn't involved in the things I was in, that I'd been alone? I found friends in school when I was there and in the hotels that I worked at. So your theory is misguided." Charles looks at his watch.

"Do you still talk to those people?" Tammy runs her thumb over the tip of her pen.

"No, we all went our own ways when I left Cunnings." Charles breaks eye contact.

"I think we just found the problem that you have," Tammy writes down the phrase "afraid of commitment" with others in the file.

"That's good, but I'll see you next week." Charles gets up out of the chair and leaves.

Tammy wakes up at around ten o'clock in the morning. As she makes her way to the bathroom to run a bath, she notices the note sitting on the table. She picks it up and reads it. She sits down at the table and starts to cry. *What happened to us?* she thinks as she cries. Looking up to see the time, she makes her way to the bedroom and changes into some clean clothes. She goes into the bathroom and cleans herself up for the day. The rest of the morning passes as Tammy does housework. Making herself lunch, she sits down at the table and eats.

After Tammy is finished eating, she put on her shoes and heads out for a walk to the Public Gardens,

Session Fourteen

"Good afternoon, Tammy. How are you?" Charles sits down in the chair after entering the office.

"I'm well, and yourself?" Tammy opens his file.

"I'm alive, so there must be a reason for it. What is the topic for today?" Charles looks out the window.

"I was thinking that since we found out what your problem is, maybe we could work on that this session." Tammy looks down at the last note that she had written the week before.

"What would that problem be? Because you didn't tell me." Charles closes his eyes.

"Your problem is that you are afraid of commitment. I think that all the abuse that you went through has stopped you from opening up to new people. To me, you look like a person that is happier being alone than with people. So tell me, how did you come to know your ex-roommates?" Tammy leans back in her chair.

"That is an interesting thought that I'm afraid of commitment. I think that I open up to people too fast, so that would be a strike on that one. However, I do prefer to be alone. The roommate story, well, I'll tell you but I think I've told you." Charles opens his eyes. "Anyway, the story goes like this. I met this black man named Charles Mayfield. I wish I had never met him now. He was a banquet server for the hotel that I work at. He came to me one day as I was reading the paper before my shift in the kitchen. He started to talk to me and I asked him if he saw what I was doing. He said that he did and then introduced himself. I told him my name and tried to get back to reading the paper. That wasn't enough of a hint for him to leave me alone, so I put the paper down and talked with him.

"I found out that he wasn't from this country and that his dream was to be an actor. Sounded like he had a plan for his future, and, well, I told him to chase his dreams and not to let someone else hold him back. I then looked at my watch and got up to start my shift early. A few days passed and then we started to talk about all types of topics at the hotel before our shifts would start because we didn't hang out outside of work. About a month later, we started to get together after work. We would drive around the city smoking weed and talking. Then one day he invited me to meet

144

these two girls that he knew. When we got to the apartment, we went in and that is when I found out that they were looking for a roommate. So after the coffee with them, Charles and I went back to my place. He told me that it would be an easy way to save money. He kept on that topic until I said that I would move in with them. A month later, I moved in with them. I then put Charles on a bus to chase his dream. He owes me over $2,000, so if I ever see him again, I'll be nice but I won't let him forget what I did for him. For some reason, all the people that I have met down here are always looking for a free ride."

"Tell me about some of them." Tammy makes a note in the file.

"What do you want to know?"

"How do you know that they are looking for a free ride?" Tammy takes a sip of her water.

"It's all in the way they hold themselves. If you are a kind person who helps a person out, like me, the person will take advantage of it and, when you stop, they get mad at you. That's how all the people I have met down here have treated me, like I owe them something for being in their presence. It doesn't matter if they are black, white, or whatever. I treat them with respect and they stab me in the back. When I stop paying their way, they all of a sudden don't have the time of day for me. I have only found that with the people down here. Out west, it doesn't matter who you are. You buy a person a beer, he or she buys the next drink." Charles glances at Tammy for a second before continuing. "It's like people don't know what the meaning of friendship is anymore down here. It's a two-way street and a real friend is someone who you can call up at any time of the day or night. Something has happened here. There are no more real friends because everyone is out for themselves. The friends that I made in Cunnings would come to the plate if needed to help me out because I had money in my pocket. But even if I didn't, they still would help. I think that my only true friend that I have left is Jen and she lives out west."

"You have just met the wrong people. There are a lot of good-hearted people here in Metro. Why do you think that people have forgotten what the meaning of friendship is?"

"They have TV, video games, computers, and the net, and that has made it so that they don't have to socialize anymore other than at work. It's sad to say but it's true. Another thing is that people are so busy with their lives that they forget to let in other people. The outcome is that when they get into a relationship with someone else, they don't know what to do. I know that you are going to tell me that I'm wrong, but I don't care. If you have friends that are real, don't take advantage of them or be taken advantage of by them." Charles looks over to the bookshelf.

"Charles, are you saying that you are giving up on meeting new people because you had some bad experiences in the past?"

"I didn't say that. I have been stabbed in the back so many times and I'm through with the pain that comes with it. You are more of a friend to me than the people that I've met down here. I think that people take my kindness as a weakness and I'm sick of it. I'm no angel because I've made my mistakes as I have grown through the years and done some bad things." Charles gets up and walks to the bookshelf. He pulls out a book, "*Dark Hearts*, this is an amazing book. It talks about how the condition of life is only held together by a thought. The author was suffering from some kind of mental illness, I can't remember what it was. Anyway, he had his star go crazy and at the end of the book he said that we all better listen because God is talking as if He has schizophrenia again." Charles puts the book back and sits back down.

"That's what that book is about. We had to study it in first-year English. It was that book that made me to want to major in psychology." Tammy taps her finger on the desk.

"You know if you want me to go, I can." Charles makes eye contact with her.

"No it's not that. It's just that you are hurt emotionally and you are giving reasons of why you are alone. Do you even want my help?" Tammy breaks eye contact.

"Like I said in the beginning, this wasn't my idea. I have been here for a few sessions now, and I'm growing to like you as someone I can talk to. The one thing that I notice is that you are always looking like you are bored with me." Charles leans back in the chair.

"It's not that. It's the fact that you have so much pain in you and you are only showing the tip, as if I'm going to hurt you more. I'm not going to hurt you; I truly want to help you."

"You don't want to hurt me. The memories that I have hurt all the time, so what does it matter if you do or don't? When I talk about the memories, they put me back in that time and the pain that I went through." Charles looks out the window again.

"Well let's talk about when you left Sova to come down here. It was your dream to move down here and I would like to hear about it."

"That was the day that I saw my dad cry because I was leaving. I'll start with the months before. My dad had sat with me and we played a game of chess. He told me that he had moved us out west for a better life and he asked me why I wanted to move back. I told him that it was my dream and that I could make it down here. We talked for a good hour-and-a-half as we played. As he put me into checkmate, he told me that it would be OK if I changed my mind. Even Jen told me to stay because she felt that I wasn't going to come back alive. The day before I left, Mom and I packed my car and she said to me that there was still time to change my mind. I said that I was going to chase my dream and that nothing would get in my way. I got up at nine on that fateful day to eat a good breakfast. I then went down to Jen's to see her one last time before I left. I gave her daughter, Sarah, a stuffed animal and a hug to her and to Jen. I got home at lunchtime from Jen's and had lunch with Mom and Dad. After lunch, I got up from the table and that is when Dad started to cry as I walked over to the door. Mom and Dad got up from the table and walked over to me to give me a hug. Then Dad said that if I decided anytime during my drive to come back home that I could. In my own mind, I was on my way home."

"Was it as hard for you?"

"I made it to the tracks just outside of town before I started to cry. I pulled the car over and sat there for about twenty minutes, crying. I got out of my car and walked onto the tracks and asked God or the higher power to watch over me. I got back into my car and drove to my brother's, which was a three-hour drive away." Charles closes his eyes.

"Do you still feel that way?"

"Sometimes, but they are only a phone call away if I need them. I talk with Mom and Dad once or twice a week, and the same with Jen. So the only difference is distance from them." Charles opens his eyes and looks down at his watch. "It's that time again, Tammy. I'll see you next week." Charles gets up and walks out of the office.

After sitting on a bench in the Public Gardens reading the paper, Tammy gets up and walks along one of the paths that lead her to the Centre Street exit. Looking both ways down Centre Street, she makes her way across to The Lord Nelson Hotel where Matt works. As she walks in the doors, she sees Matt in the restaurant sitting at the table with another cook. She makes her way to a booth and sits down.

"Can I help you?" a server asks.

"I'd like a cup of coffee and a menu. As well, could you let Matt know that Tammy is here in the restaurant?" Tammy points Matt out.

"I will let him know and I'll be back with your coffee and menu," says the server.

A few minutes pass before the server returns with the coffee and menu. "Matt said that he will be here in a couple of minutes. Do you know what you want or do you need a few minutes?" The server hands Tammy the menu.

"I will have the spinach salad with a bowl of the roasted butternut squash soup." Tammy hands the menu back to the server.

As Tammy waits for her food, Matt comes to the table. "I'm working, what do you need?" Matt sets his hands on the table.

"I think I'm going to spend the night at my parents." Tammy looks up at Matt.

"OK. I'll call you there after I get home from work at around seven. I'll talk to you then." Matt leaves the table.

A few minutes later, the server brings Tammy her food. "Is there anything else that I can get for you?"

"I forgot to ask if it could be to-go—is that OK?" Tammy smiles to the server.

"Not a problem. I'll get your bill and box this up for you." the server picks the food up from the table. As the server returns with the box, she hands Tammy the bill for $17.95.

"Here is a twenty; keep the change." Tammy gets up from the table and makes her way outside the hotel and gets into a waiting taxi.

"Where to, lady?" the taxi driver asks.

"Thirteen fifty seventh Maple Street," Tammy closes the door.

The taxi driver turned the meter on and drives out of the driveway of the hotel. It was a ten-minute drive from the hotel to her parents. As the taxi driver stops at the address, he says, "That will be fifteen bucks please."

Tammy gives the cab driver the money and opens the door. She walks up to the door and opens it. "Tammy, come in. Would you like something to eat?" Dr. Maxwell had seen the taxi and met Tammy at the door.

"No, I got some food from the hotel. Is it OK that I stay here tonight? Matt and I had a fight the other night and I need some time to myself. He is going to be calling tonight, so you or Mom can tell him that I'm sleeping or something." Tammy takes off her shoes.

"You shouldn't be like that. Your mother and I had our fights when we were younger, but we always talked about it. When he calls, I think that you should talk to him, and if you still want to spend the night you can." Dr. Maxwell closes the door.

"I don't know, Dad. For the last few months after Matt got his promotion, he has spent more time at the hotel than ever before." Tammy walks into the living room and sits down. "It's like he is more interested in working than being at home with me."

"You know, Tammy, before you were born, your mother and I hardly saw each other because I was busy at the hospital and she was in school all the time. The time that we had together was a few hours a day and, for the first part, we were always fighting. One day we sat down at the table and talked about the problem and decided that the time that we would spend together would be quality time." Dr. Maxwell sits down on the sofa. "It was then that we saw our relationship change. We didn't fight any more and, during those few hours we spent, we would go for walks, watch movies, and talk about what we wanted from the relationship. Then you came into our lives. Our lives changed again, but we talked and we haven't had a fight in many years. Now we talk about when I'll be calling it quits at the hospital, and when that happens, our lives will change again. That's what happens when you talk instead of fighting."

"Dad, our situation is different." Tammy rests her arms on the chair.

"Tell me how it's different. Are you cheating on him?" Dr. Maxwell looks at Tammy.

"No, I'm not cheating. It's different because when I look into his eyes, I think I see that he wants to be out of the relationship. When we talk, we talk about the future, but I don't think that he means it or wants it." Tammy starts to sob.

"Tammy, it's OK. If he didn't mean it, he wouldn't say it. I know that it's hard for you, but I think that it's just as hard on him. When I see you two together, I can tell that he really loves you.

Take it from me, if he wanted out of the relationship he would have already left you." Dr. Maxwell gets to his feet and walks into the kitchen. "Would you like a coffee?"

"Sure." Tammy wipes the tears from her eyes. "Where's Mom?"

"She is at one of her art meetings. She should be home in a few hours." Dr. Maxwell walks back into the living room with the coffees. He hands Tammy a cup.

"Dad, when did you know that Mom was the one for you?" Tammy takes a sip of her coffee.

"Well, it would have been the third date and I knew then. She struck me as an angel and she said that this date will last the rest of our lives and, for the most part, it has. So when Matt calls, talk to him, and go from there." Dr. Maxwell sits back down.

"OK, Dad. I will." Tammy puts the coffee cup on the table. "He wrote me a letter saying that he was sorry about the fight last night. He said that he had a bad day at work and he was sorry for taking it out on me." Tammy shakes her head.

"That happens from time to time. I have my bad days, so does your mother, and you probably have had them, too. So I can give you a ride home after you talk to Matt and, as I said, if you still want to stay here, you can." Dr. Maxwell picks up the remote for the TV.

"It must be five, right?" Tammy takes another sip of her coffee.

"I only watch the news to know what is happening in the world. It's your mother who watches all the shows, but at five I get the TV for an hour." Dr. Maxwell smiles and turns to face the TV.

"Dad, I'm going to eat and then lay down. If I'm asleep when Matt calls, wake me." Tammy gets up from the chair and goes to her bedroom.

"I will." Dr. Maxwell turns his attention to the news.

Seven o'clock comes to pass and there is no phone call from Matt. As eight o'clock approaches, the phone rings. It's Matt. Dr. Maxwell talks to him for a few minutes before waking Tammy. He hands her the phone. Tammy and Matt talk for about an hour before she tells him that she will be coming home and then hangs up.

"Dad, can I get that ride home?" Tammy asks as she walks into the living room and hands him the phone.

"Sure, give me a second to put my shoes on and then we will be on our way." Dr. Maxwell gets up from where he was sitting.

They make their way out to the car in the driveway. They get in and Tammy's dad starts the car. "Dad, do dreams come true?"

"All dreams come true, you just have to work for them. They come true without our even knowing. Every day on the ward I see patients who have lost all hope for their life. I always tell them that the illness that they have shouldn't hold them back from reaching their dreams and goals, no matter how big they are. The only downfall is that they don't think like that. I have this one patient who writes music and she is only in her early twenties. She sits at the piano in the activity room all day. I asked her what her dream was and she said it was to be able to be loved by a man so she could raise a family. All dreams, if you want them to come true, come true." Dr. Maxwell starts driving down the street.

"How many patients do you have that believe you?" Tammy asks as she watches the houses pass by.

"That's hard to answer because some do and some don't. They are ones who do recover faster because they see the light of hope at the end of the tunnel and they go forward. On the other hand, the others only see the bad and the illness. Most of the time, they are in for months at a time. I just try to give a positive attitude and outlook for my patients. These are things that you should be using with your clients." Dr. Maxwell makes a right turn onto South Street, turns left onto Morris Street and pulls up to her house. "You know, Tammy, life is funny. At the moment, you are going through a bad patch and it will pass. You just have to be strong enough to weather the storm. Have a good night dear."

"Good night, Dad." Tammy opens the door and waves as her father pulls away. She looks up and sees the sky in a dark shade of orange. Opening the door of the condo, she walked in.

Matt is sitting on the step. "I talked to Chef today and he said that if I need some time off, he would let me take it." Matt gets to his feet.

"You didn't have to do that." Tammy takes off her shoes and puts them away.

"I haven't taken a holiday in three years, so he said it would be fine," Matt says, as Tammy comes up the stairs.

"So when are you thinking of taking the time?" Tammy puts her arms around Matt to give him a hug.

"Starting in the morning I'm going to be off for three weeks. So I'm thinking that on Friday after you're done work, that we head to the South Shore and stay at White Point Beach Resort. What do you think?" Matt hugs her.

"Let's think about it. All I want to do is to have a shower and go to bed." Tammy kisses him.

"Sounds like a plan." Matt kisses her back.

Tammy makes her way to the bathroom. Matt walks back into the living room and puts in a movie. He can hear the running of water in the shower. His mind drifts from the movie and he falls asleep in the chair.

CHAPTER nine

Tammy wakes up to the crackle of thunder from a storm that rolled in during the night. Looking to see the time on the clock radio on her nightstand, she sees it's 5:30. She can hear the rain on the window and the snoring of Matt beside her. Reaching up to the clock, she turns the alarm off and rolls out of bed. She walks out of the bedroom in her nightdress and into the kitchen. Putting on a pot of coffee, she opens the fridge to get some eggs and finds only three of them. Setting them on the counter, she gets a frying pan out from the stove. She turns the burner on, places the frying pan on it and cracks the eggs into it.

Tammy pulls out a plate and fork from the dishwasher, and sets them on the counter beside the stove. She goes over to the sink, washes out her coffee cup from the day before, and fills it. Turning back to the eggs, she flips them and then puts them onto her plate. She picks up the plate and her coffee, walks over to the table, and sits down. She seasons her eggs with salt and pepper and starts to eat.

This Monday is just like all the rest that have come and gone in the last few years. She is always up before six. But today is two days before Charles is to return. That is what's on her mind this morning—not the rain she would have to walk in to get to work or the fact that Matt was starting his holidays. "Charles," she says, out loud. "What has happened to you?" She knows that there was something to make him return to her. Maybe he just wanted to say goodbye before leaving Metro—or was he the patient that her father had talked about the other Sunday? She didn't know. Then all the memories of him come back.

Looking up at the time and seeing that it's 6:20, Tammy gets up from the table, puts her dishes in the sink, and returns to the bedroom to pick out what she will wear for work. With clothes in arm, she makes her way to the bathroom to shower. She exits the bathroom and heads for the bedroom, where Matt is still asleep. She moves close to the bed and kisses him on the head. Turning, she makes her way out of the bedroom to the stairs. She puts on her rain jacket.

Tammy opens the door and leaves for work. As she walks up the street in the rain, she stops in at The News to pick up her paper and a cup of coffee. "Good morning Rob," Tammy says, approaching the counter.

"Well, hello, Tammy. How are you on this fine morning?" Rob rings in her coffee and paper.

"I'm doing well. This is some storm that we are having." Tammy pulls out her change purse.

"It is nice to get the rain where it has been so nice for the last few days. Your total today is $3.50." Tammy puts the money on the counter. "Thanks, Tammy. Have a good day."

"Thank you, and the same to you." Tammy leaves the shop.

Tammy gets to her office as the rain lightens up to just a drizzle. She takes off her rain jacket, sits down behind her desk, and opens the paper. About an hour passes before Carolin shows up.

"Good morning Tammy." Carolin pokes her head into Tammy's office as she hangs her rain jacket on the coat hanger behind her desk.

"Good morning, Carolin."

"How did yesterday go?" Carolin sits down in one of the leather chairs in the office.

"It was a day in the life of Matt's and my relationship." Tammy closes the paper and passes it to Carolin.

"What happened?" Carolin takes the paper.

"We had a fight Saturday night and, well, on Sunday when I woke up, Matt left me a note. It made me think about all of those other times when we had fought." Tammy looks to the top of her desk.

"Don't tell me you broke up." Carolin's mouth drops.

"No, we didn't break up, but it took my dad to pick up the pieces with me. Carolin, we help people through their problems, but we can't seem to find the way through ours. Why is that?" Tammy makes eye contact.

"We're human, too, and we have our own problems outside of work. That's why many people wonder how people like us, in this field of work, manage every day after listening to other people's problems. Some use drugs to drift away, others use alcohol and drink themselves into an early grave. We all have problems, Tammy, and that's what makes us human." Carolin leans back to break eye contact.

"How are we to help others when we can't even help ourselves?" Tammy turns and looks out the window.

"It's what we do, Tammy. It's like our life is in total chaos and we are able to help others to get away from theirs. You know what I mean?" Carolin yawns.

"I guess."

"Well, let's help some of the members of society get on with their lives." Carolin gets up from the chair and leaves Tammy's office.

Session Fifteen

The door of Tammy's office opens and Charles walks in. "Good afternoon, Tammy." He takes a seat. "What is the plan for me today? We have covered my life in a nutshell, so what is next?"

"How do you handle your feelings when you get upset?" Tammy opens up his file.

"I deal with it like everyone else. I lose my temper and people start to run. That's how I deal with it." Charles makes eye contact.

"So you blow up. How often have you lost your temper at work?" Tammy makes a note.

"Maybe five or six times since I started working at the hotel. Why?" Charles asks with a look of confusion on his face.

"I'm trying to find out why your boss would want you to get counselling. How does your father handle himself when he is upset?"

"He yells and, well, we all run for cover in the house. Why do you ask?" Charles looks out the window.

"Because if your father can't control his emotions, how are you going to learn? If your father yells and everyone runs for cover, then you have a greater chance to follow in his footsteps. How about your mother?" Tammy takes a sip of her water.

"Mom, she keeps it bottled up inside and when she goes off, it is normal for my father to go off at the same time. So they start to fight." Charles closes his eyes and leans back.

"Did your parents fight lots when you were growing up?"

"Yeah, but whose parents don't fight?" Charles opens his eyes.

"How often would they fight?" Tammy tries to push Charles to a boiling point.

"I don't know. I was always biking or working at the restaurant, so I was only at home for a short time during the day when we lived in Prussia. In the winter, I would be walking instead of biking, just to let you know." Charles glances at Tammy, letting her know that his blood pressure is rising.

"When your parents were mad, would they take it out on you or your brother or sister?"

"It didn't matter. If you were in the line of fire, you would get the brunt of it." Charles's face starts showing his discomfort with Tammy's questions.

"Charles, do your parents drink?"

"What is this? Blame my parents because I lose my temper and blow up, as you like to put it. My parents aren't perfect." Charles starts leaning toward the desk.

"Charles answer the question, do your parents drink?" Tammy asks again.

"What? Do you want to know that my dad is an alcoholic and uses it to drown out his past as a child? Do you also want to know that he was beat by his stepdad and that's why he never hit us? Do you want to know that, when he was eleven, his stepdad died in a car accident? Do you want to know that his mother put him and his brothers in an orphanage because she couldn't afford to keep them? Do you want to know that my dad hasn't even finished high school? Do you want to know that everything my parents do is for us kids first? What is it? Tell me," Charles shoots back with anger in this monotone voice.

"Charles, you don't have to get upset. I only asked a simple question."

"So, what do you want to know? Do you want to know that I wasn't breathing for five minutes after I was born? Do you want to know that I have seen my father cry? Do you want to know that my parents came up from getting by, by the skin of their teeth? Tammy what is it? Answer me!" Charles slams his hand on the arm of the chair.

"Charles, calm down. You don't have to get your defenses up. They are just questions. Take a deep breath and relax." Realizing she has lost all control of the session, she tries to calm him.

"Breathe. I'll tell you what, you write a note to my chef saying that I'm fine and that I don't need to come back." Charles gets up from the chair. "I'll see you next week, and you better have the letter ready for me," he says, walking out the door of the office.

"It's not that easy," Tammy calls, as Charles walks out. All he does is turns back to glare at her before walking out of the office completely.

As lunch approaches, Tammy finishes off her morning sessions with her clients. Walking out of her office, she looks at Carolin. "Lunchtime."

"Are we just staying in the building?" Carolin gets up.

"Yeah, the rain is still coming down and it is right here." Tammy starts for the door.

Tammy and Carolin go down to the main-floor restaurant. They get a table, and a waiter brings them both a water and menu. After about five minutes, he returned to get their order. "What would you ladies like for lunch?"

"I'll have the Smoked Salmon Sandwich with salad," says Tammy, handing him the menu.

"What kind of dressing for the salad?"

"I'll have the balsamic herb," Tammy says, and smiles.

"OK, and what would you like?" The waiter turns to look at Carolin.

"I'll have the lemon dill chicken salad." Carolin hands him the menu.

"Is the water fine for the both of you?" asks the waiter as he puts the menu that Carolin gave him under his arm with Tammy's.

Both Tammy and Carolin say, yes, that the water is fine. The waiter leaves the table to the kitchen to place the order.

"Carolin, in the last three years we have gotten more clients and, for the most part, we have helped them. Some have moved on, and others continue to come back week after week. Now, after saying that, we have changed the way we approach each one of them and I'm thinking that we'll need to expand. There is another office where we hold our files, so let's clean it out and either get another psychologist or find someone to replace you and you can use your schooling as a counsellor. What do you think?" Tammy makes eye contact with Carolin.

"I think it is a good idea. I think that we can go to MDI to find someone to do my job and then we will be set." Carolin smiles because that is what she has wanted for the past three years. She turns to look out the window and says, "Finally" under her breath.

"That's a good idea to use MDI. I think that we should call the school and ask if they have anyone who is looking for a job."

The rain falls in a way that would make a person remember when they were a young child playing in it. It delivered a calming peace to the city. Tammy's and Carolin's food arrives and they set in a comfortable silence as they eat. "You know, I miss this, Tammy," Carolin finally says, breaking the silence.

"Miss what?"

"Comfortable silences. It's rare for us, but it is nice when we can sit together in peace and quiet." Carolin takes a sip of her water.

"Yeah, and you had to break it," Tammy laughs.

The waiter comes back to the table with the bill and Tammy pays it.

Session Sixteen

Charles enters Tammy's office and sits down in one of the chairs in front of her desk. "Do you have the letter ready?"

"I do, but there are a few things I want to say before I give it to you. I think that you should reconsider not coming back. We have only touched the tip of the iceberg that is who you are. I feel that there is an underlying mental illness that is trying to take over your life. As well, I feel that you could benefit from more counselling to help you to deal with your past in Prussia." Tammy opens up the file.

"Who are you trying to fool? An underlying mental illness, my past—who do you think you are to tell me that? It's my life, if I had a mental illness, I think I would know." Charles angrily shakes his head.

"You wouldn't know if you had a mental illness because it's something that, if you deal with it on your own by drinking or doing drugs, it wouldn't show. I think that a psychiatric evaluation with a psychiatrist would help because there is only so much I can do. I know that you do suffer from something, but I don't know what. So do yourself a favour and get the help you need." Tammy closes the file.

"The letter." Charles rolls his eyes and reaches out with his right hand.

"Here, take it. If you want to come back any time, the door is open." Tammy hands him the letter.

Five o'clock hits, and Tammy's last patient leaves the office. She walks into the waiting room and pulls up a chair in front of Carolin. "Did you get a minute to call the school with the job opportunity?"

"I did, and they told me that they have a student who's going to be ready for the work experience part of her course on Monday." Carolin closes out her computer.

"Well what else did you say?"

"I said that she should come and see us. So, they are going to get her to stop by tomorrow at 12:30 to talk with us." Carolin gets up from behind her desk.

"That's good. We will be able to see her work and be able to see if she will fit in. Are you ready to go home?" Tammy stands up.

Just then, the door opens and Matt walks in with a teddy bear in one hand and a red rose in the other. "Hi, Carolin. Tammy, these are for you." Matt hands her the teddy bear and rose.

"Well, look at you. I haven't seen you in some time, Matt. I guess that I will be on my way home. Tammy, I'll see you in the morning." Carolin gets her raincoat.

"We'll give you a ride, Carolin." Tammy puts her arms around Matt.

"Yeah, so wait a second." Matt gives Tammy a kiss.

It's still raining as the three of them get into Matt's car. Matt starts the engine, turns down the music, and asks, "Carolin, where do you live again?"

"In Clayton Park, by the mall." Carolin put son her seatbelt.

"You'll have to tell me when to turn when I get there." Matt puts the car into gear and heads to Clayton Park, which is a good fifteen-minute drive away if the traffic is light, but it is rush hour.

It takes them half an hour to get to the mall and another five minutes to get to Carolin's townhouse. "If you guys want, you can come in for a coffee," Carolin says, as she gets out of the car.

"It's up to you, Matt," Tammy pokes Matt.

"I guess we could come in for one." Matt shuts off the car.

Tammy and Matt walk up to the front door of Carolin's place. Matt locks the car with his remote and put his keys into his pocket while Carolin unlocks and opens the door. The three of them walk in and Matt, being last, closes the door.

"I get the coffee going and I'll order a pizza for us to eat." Carolin takes off her shoes. She walks to the kitchen, starts the coffee, and picks up the phone to call Alexandra's Pizza, a local pizza place in Clayton Park.

"Did you just move into this place, Carolin?" Matt walks into the living room.

"No, I bought it two years ago." Carolin sets a plate of cookies on the coffee table and sits down in the living room with them.

"That would make sense, because the last time I was over at your place you were still living in an apartment downtown. That would have been about two-and-a-half years ago." Matt sits down in one of the chairs around the coffee table.

"I thought that you were here before." Carolin turns on some background music.

"Maybe, I can't remember, but that could have happened. At least you are in a good area of town—not like us with all the traffic going up and down Morris and the hospital and fire department being down the street, too." Matt picks up a cookie.

"It's not that bad, Matt. We live downtown. We are where the action is." Tammy takes a seat on the sofa.

"Yeah, 200 bars, twenty hotels, all types of restaurants and shops. Not to mention fifteen office towers, apartment buildings, and government buildings all around the downtown," Matt says, with a hint of dislike for the condo.

"Matt, let's not get into this here. I know that you don't like living downtown, but we are close to work and most of our friends." Tammy looks at Matt.

"Yeah, and don't leave out all the noisy university students that live in our area. But we won't talk about it. Maybe we will sell and move out to an area like this in the future." Matt shakes his head.

"MATT! That's enough, we are here to have coffee not to get into a fight about where we live." Tammy raises her voice and makes eye contact with him.

"OK. Sorry, Carolin. Just saying I like where you are living. How was the day for you?" Matt turns his attention to her.

"It was good. Tammy and I are going to hire a new assistant and I'll be counselling patients, too." Carolin smiles and continues. "The coffee should be just about done; I'll go and get it. Matt what do you take in your coffee?"

"Two cream and two sugar will be fine. Or black it really doesn't matter." Matt looks back to Tammy.

Carolin comes in with the coffees. The three of them sit in the living room and talk for hours about everything and anything. As nine o'clock hits, Tammy and Matt leave Carolin's to head home. By this time the rain has stopped and the clouds have cleared off to show a full moon. As Tammy and Matt get to the condo, Matt unlocks the door and walks in with Tammy behind him. Taking off his boots, he heads to the kitchen to make a pot of coffee.

"Didn't you drink enough at Carolin's? I'm sure you have been drinking it all day," Tammy says, passing the door of the kitchen where Matt is standing.

"I did. Caffeine is my drug of choice and I have to get as much as I can." Matt smiles at her.

"At least it's not booze or smoking anything." Tammy walks into the kitchen to see a bottle of rum on the counter. "Are you putting that in your coffee?"

"No, why do you ask?" Matt picks the bottle up.

"Why is there a bottle of rum here then?" Tammy makes eye contact with him.

"It's for you and it is coconut rum," Matt opens the cupboard where they keep their booze and puts it there.

"Oh." Tammy turns away and walks out of the kitchen.

Matt pours a coffee for himself and heads into the living room. Sitting down in his chair, he turns on some music and picks up the book he'd started to read earlier that day. Tammy comes out of the bedroom and sits down on the arm of his chair. "What do you want, Tammy?"

"I want to know what you are doing, that's all." Tammy places her hand on his chest.

"I'm reading this book that I picked up at the bookstore across from the hotel. It's called *The Gift*. It's about this guy that is down on his luck and tries to take his own life, but is met with historical figures who give him pieces of paper with writing on them that he is to read. That is what it says on the back of the book. So far, I have gotten to the point when he is just about to shoot himself in the head. What are you doing?" Matt turns his attention to Tammy.

"I'm wanting my boyfriend to come to bed, that's all." Tammy starts to rub his chest. "If you come to bed, I'll give you a back rub and something else."

"Well, if you put it that way." Matt sets the book down on the coffee table. He gets up and follows Tammy to the bedroom.

CHAPTER ten

It is six in the morning when the alarm goes off, waking both Tammy and Matt. Tammy reaches over to the nightstand and turns it off. She rolls out of bed and notices that Matt has fallen back to sleep. Making her way to the kitchen, she starts a pot of coffee. She walks over to the window that faces east to see the sun rise with its reds, oranges, and yellows over the harbour. Turning, she goes to the bathroom and gets ready for work.

After about twenty minutes, Tammy comes out ready for work. She walks into the kitchen, pours herself a cup of coffee, grabs a yogurt from the fridge, and sits down at the table. As she eats her yogurt and drinks her coffee, she looks at the bookshelf that holds all of Matt's cookbooks. She gets up from her chair and walks over to them. Picking one out of about fifty, she flips it open and starts to look for a meal that Matt maybe will make her for supper. She finds one that is a chicken breast stuffed with goat cheese, basil, and sundried tomatoes, and finished with a roasted red bell pepper cream sauce. She makes a note to Matt that she would like it if he could make that for supper and that she will stop at the liquor store to pick up a bottle of wine.

Looking up at the time, Tammy heads out. She stops at The News for a paper and another cup of coffee.

"Coffee today, Tammy?" Rob asks as she approaches the counter.

"Yeah, I'm still trying to wake up." Tammy sets the paper on the counter.

"Coffee is on me, just the paper, so that is a buck-fifty." Rob smiles.

"Thanks Rob. It's a nice morning," Tammy says, handing him the money.

"It is. Have a good day, Tammy, and I'll see you tomorrow morning." Rob smiles as Tammy leaves the store.

It is almost eight o'clock when Tammy gets to her office. Sitting down in her chair, she starts to read the paper. Fifteen minutes pass before Carolin shows up for work. Looking up, Tammy sees her coming through the door and sitting down in one of the chairs. "Good morning Carolin, how are you today?" Tammy sets the paper down.

"Not bad, and you?" Carolin makes eye contact.

"Well, I'm still breathing so that must mean that I'm well," Tammy laughs. "You'll never guess what I did this morning."

"Used your lipstick as a tampon and tried to use the tampon as lipstick," Carolin says, with a straight face.

"No, silly. I left Matt a note to make me supper tonight."

"That's cool. Will he do it, is the question. So, last night after you guys left, I picked up one of my psychology magazines and read an article about how that the people who suffer from mental illness are pushed out of sight by society like they don't even matter. We put them in hospitals, boarding homes, and such in the hope that the problem will just go away. It's sad. They say that three percent of the world suffers from mental illness."

"I think that you have mentioned that a few days ago, but go on." Tammy leans back.

"Tammy, three percent. It is a small number, but when you look at the whole world of six billion or so people, that's about 180 million people worldwide. Here is a question for you: why, when we were in high school, didn't we learn about mental illness, but they taught us about every other illness in health class. Why is that?"

"I don't know. Do you know?"

"I don't know, either. I feel that it should be taught, but it's not. It's time for us as a society to stop living in the dark ages about mental illness. Today, they said that most doctors overmedicate their patients who suffer from mental illness. They also have done experiments on them to see if that would help them. It's barbaric, what we do. We alienate them, drug them, and try experiments on them. When is it going to stop? When is the human race going to accept them and not push them away?" Carolin shakes her head.

"I don't know if it will ever change. We live in a world that is ignorant toward the mentally ill and most people believe that if they can't see it, it's not there. That's the kind of world we live in, and there's nothing that you or I can do to change it."

"I know. If there was only some way to spread the message about the treatment to the world community about what happens. One way is to educate people while they are still in school, and I don't mean university or college. It has to start in high school."

"Dad has always taught me that people try to understand cancer and other illnesses, and broken bones, because these are things they can see or relate to, but they don't want to try to understand mental illness since they can't see or relate to it." Tammy looks down to the paper on her desk.

"Is it because they don't want to, or is it that they are ignorant?" Carolin turns and looks out the window.

"Dad never told me why that was." Tammy looks at the clock on the wall. "You know, Charles comes back tomorrow."

"I know. Don't change the subject, Tammy. As counsellors, we are on the front line of this because we deal with them every day." She runs her hand through her hair.

"Carolin, look. Here in Metro, we have a mental hospital on the other side of the harbour plus the Abbey over here where dad works. We are only a city of 500,000 at best, before you count the university and college student. And during the summer, there are the tourists to consider. For the most part, this country only has 32 million people from coast to coast. What are we in that equation?"

"You know, one man had a dream and it was standardized time. It happened and he was from this country. So anything is possible."

"Yeah, that's right. But why don't you mention the man who invented insulin then? He was from this country, too. Carolin, don't get me wrong. I understand what you are saying, but I wouldn't know where to start."

"We could start by educating the public through workshops here in Metro and inviting people from other cities to be part of them. That way, they would do the same in their cities, and then it might spread out around the world like wildfire."

"That has been tried already and the people who went were the people from the mental health wards and that was it. We could try. If you want, I can talk to my dad tonight about the idea and see what he says." Tammy looks at the time and sees that it is almost nine. "It's time to look alive because, it's almost nine."

Back at Tammy and Matt's condo, Matt is just getting up. Looking at the clock, Matt changes into his jeans and a white tee shirt. As he makes his way out to the kitchen, he sees the pot of coffee that is still on. He pours a cup, gets some cereal, and sits down at the table where he sees Tammy's note. *Make supper. Yeah, OK*, Matt thinks. Finishing his breakfast, he takes his bowl to the sink and pours out his coffee. He walks to the closet, pulls out his leather coat, and puts it on. Sitting down on the steps, he laces up his black army boots. He puts on his baseball hat while opening the door, then turns and locks it. He then leaves the condo and walks up to the News to get a paper.

"Good day Rob, how are you on this day?" Matt puts the paper on the counter.

"Not bad, Matt. Need smokes today?" Rob rings in the paper.

"I do." Matt pulls out his wallet.

"That comes to $10.75. Need matches?"

"No, have a good day Rob." Matt walks out of the door to the sidewalk.

He makes his way down to the boardwalk that circles the waterfront of the harbour. He finds a bench to sit on and lights up a smoke from his pack. He reads the paper's food section and then the headlines of the main section. About two smokes later, he read the funnies in the back. When he finishes, he rolls the paper up and puts it in the garbage can beside the bench. He gets up and starts down the boardwalk to the other end of downtown.

As Matt gets to Grandville Street where all the bikers usually park their hogs, he notices that there are none parked. He opens the door of French, a coffee shop owned by one of his friends, and finds there's no line like at other coffee shops in the area.

"Matt are you on holidays? That's the word around the campfire." The man behind the counter puts out his hand.

"That would be the truth. How's it going, Dave?" Matt takes his hand.

"Not bad. How are your holidays?" Dave grabs a cup. "Coffee, Matt?"

"That's what I came in for."

"Well, let's sit down and get caught up." Dave pours two cups of coffee then comes out from behind the counter and calls for his assistant to wait on customers.

Matt makes his way to one of the tables by the windows. "Dave, looks like you're not doing so well in the coffee business. Maybe you should come back to cooking." Dave hands him his coffee.

"No, I'm doing very well. This is the slow time in the day for me. From six to about eight-thirty, it is nuts in here. And then by nine, not a soul or the odd person walks in. Ten-thirty hits and it doesn't end until we close." Dave sits down. "I told you a couple of years ago about doing this with me, and you said that you would make more money cooking."

"I did, I know, but I'm still sticking to my decision." Matt takes a sip of his coffee. "You know, Dave, we have been friends since college or cooking school whatever you want to call it."

"You mean three years of being drunk." Dave smiles.

"It was three years? I only remember two. But anyway, I was thinking of putting up a restaurant in this area. I mean in Metro." Matt looks out the window.

"It would be a good idea with your talent, but on the other hand, seven out of every ten restaurants fail in the first year alone. You have to look at both sides of the coin. Where would you be looking?"

"There is an old townhouse down from the hotel that was once a restaurant. It's pink now, but a paint job can solve that."

"I know where you are talking about. It would be easier to do something new because you can place things where you want them. You know what I mean? If it was a coffee shop, you really don't need to do new—something like that building is over 200 years old. So, anyway, how are you and Tammy doing? You have never told me the story behind you two."

"We're doing well. Now that I'm on holidays, we'll find out. When you work in a hotel, you always know when you start, but you don't know when you go home." Matt takes another drink.

"That's why I didn't work in hotels. The time together will help. My girlfriend always comes in for a coffee before work every day, and I'm normally back at my place by seven at the latest unless something happens."

"You don't live with her, do you? They are different if you live with them, trust me. Three years ago, I moved in with Tammy because she needed a roommate. That's how it started. In other words, that is how she hooked me. I was only focused on work and had just started at the hotel. She was busy with her life but wanted a boyfriend. She didn't like going to clubs alone so her friends, one in particular, would set her up with a male friend. You know her too because she is one of your exes. Good system, you would think. But anyway, I had met with Tammy a couple of times with Carolin, your ex, at the condo. I thought that it was in a perfect location for me for work, and, well, the clubs."

"Good point. You just live up by me, just off Morris. It must have been hard to bring anyone home." Dave watches a customer walk in.

"Yeah," Matt laughs. "For the first two months, our times of being awake didn't match. She was always asleep when I would get home from work and I was asleep when she would leave for work. But then there were the weekends when she didn't work and would be at home. My weekends were always Monday and Tuesday, and I was always out doing things. Then one Friday night, I came home drunk to a candle party happening in the condo that I knew nothing about. Carolin pulled me aside and told me that Tammy liked me and that I should ask her out some time. That's how it started."

"Wasn't that nice. It was a set-up and you were the sucker," Dave snickers. "If a woman ever tries something like that, I won't bite. You should have seen that coming a mile away."

"Yeah, I got to get running and you got to get ready. So, Dave, I'll see you later and feel free to stop by for a coffee." Matt gets up from the table, walks out the door, and lights a smoke. He heads down to Barrington toward the farmers market.

Matt reaches the market fifteen minutes later, and walks in the sliding doors. He picks up a basket and starts shopping for the menu that Tammy wants for supper. As he's about to leave, he picks up a food magazine, as well. He makes his way out of the market and heads home up one of the hills that makes up most of Metro. By the time he gets home, it's started to cloud over and the wind starts to roll off the harbour.

Matt makes his way to the kitchen, puts the food on the counter, and starts to prepare the chicken and sauce. Looking up to the clock on the oven, he sees that it is 11:50. He continues to stuff the chicken.

There is just something that Matt can't get away from and it is cooking at home or at work. It's been his life since he was eleven years old when he started to help his parents in their restaurant. Now at the age of thirty, he is second in command in one of the top hotels in Metro. The only thing that he doesn't like about his job is the hours. The one thing that he wants more than the chef job at the hotel is to have his own restaurant. That is his dream.

The things that Matt found out about himself over the years were that he has to keep moving forward and learning new things. His time in school was a short three years that had taught him the fundamentals of cooking and the business side of it.

The biggest thing that Matt wants in his life, though, is a family, and with Tammy, he feels that he found someone who could be the mother of his children. So when they have their fights or bad days, he always sees them through and tries to make things right.

When the clock hits noon, Matt cleans up, puts the chicken in the fridge and takes the sauce off the heat. He puts on his sandals, heads out the door, and lights up another smoke en route across the street to the Chinese restaurant for the lunch special, an all-you-can-eat buffet.

By this time, Tammy and Carolin are making their way to the café on the main floor of their building for lunch. As they walk in, they take a seat beside the window. A couple minutes pass before a waiter brings both of them menus and water.

"We know the menu, we don't need it anymore," Carolin says to the waiter with a laugh.

"Well, then, I'll tell you that we start a new menu on Monday. So when I see you two come in until then, I'll just bring you water and you can tell me what you want to eat." The waiter smiles. "Ladies, what would you like today for lunch?"

"I'll have the chicken wrap with salad and the balsamic dressing." Carolin hands the menu to him.

"I'll have the special with soup that is on the board." Tammy hands the menu to him.

"Not a problem, ladies." The waiter walks away to place the order.

"Tammy, for the past three years we have been coming here for lunch and he has always been our waiter and we don't even know his name." Carolin makes eye contact.

"His name is Michael. He's a friend of Matt's."

"Why doesn't he call you by your name, then?" Carolin picks up her glass of water.

"It's just how he is. His family runs this café." Tammy watches the cars passing by.

"Is he single and how old is he?" Carolin takes a drink of water.

"Carolin, always with that question. He is single and he is the same age as Matt. They've known each other since they were four or five. His family moved down here when he was that age and, when Matt came back here for work, they got back together again. Small world." Tammy looks back at Carolin.

"I wonder why Matt never mentioned him to me when I was looking for a boyfriend."

"Do you want to date all of Matt's friends? Remember Dave? You know the one that you were seeing when Matt moved into the condo with me? Over the years, you've had so many boyfriends it's hard to count them all. For a while there, you would have two or three a month. When are you going to find the one for you and settle down?" Tammy picks the napkin up and wipes the corner of her mouth.

"I don't know. I just like playing the field. And I only dated Dave unless Matt only has two friends," Carolin laughs. "You know there are so many guys out there and I don't think that Metro has the man for me."

"Come on, you know that there are plenty of nice guys here, you just have to look for them."

"Then there is you, getting all of your friends to set you up with their male friends. Look at Matt, a friend of mine, when you were looking for something serious, you looked for a roommate. You played the field in a different way. So, I'm just not ready to settle down." Carolin picks up the fork just before their order is set in front of them.

After lunch, Tammy and Carolin make their way back to the office for the rest of the day. By this time Matt has left the Chinese restaurant and headed to the Public Gardens for a walk. Making his way through the gates, he walks over to the pond to feed the swans and ducks. After running out of feed, he walks around the border of the fence to the path that leads around the inside of the Gardens.

Matt leaves the Public Gardens and heads down Spring Garden Road to the bookstore. He looks at the bargain table for cookbooks to see that he already has them all. Then one book captures his eye: *The Gates*. He picks it up, reads the last chapter quickly, and decides to buy it. Before going to pay, he walks down to the cooking section to look and see if there is anything there that would catch his attention. Nothing does.

Matt leaves the bookstore and heads down to the Midtown Theatres to see what's playing that night. He pulls out a pad of paper and his pen and writes down the movies. His idea is that after supper he will take Tammy out to a movie. He returns the pad of paper to his pocket and heads home.

Back at the condo, he does some cleaning before sitting in his chair, lighting a smoke and turning on the TV to get caught up on some news around the world. When the news starts to repeat, he turns the TV off and picks up the book that he's already reading.

As five o'clock arrives, Matt gets up and starts cooking supper. Fifteen minutes later, Tammy comes home from work. "Supper will be another twenty minutes because of the rice," Matt says as Tammy walks into the kitchen to smell the hint of garlic and roasted peppers sautéeing in butter.

"Smells good. I thought that a sweet white wine would go well with the chicken." Tammy hands the wine to Matt.

"You chose a sweet wine, nice. It will go great with the chicken, which is almost cooked. How was your day?" Matt pours the cream into the pan with the garlic and peppers.

"It was good. You know your friend Michael? Is he single?" Tammy opens the oven to see the chicken.

"Who's asking? Wait, let me guess, is it Carolin?" Matt closes the oven on Tammy. "It's almost done."

"Yeah, it was Carolin." Tammy opens up the cupboard to get the plates down.

"He is far from single. He and Nichol are in the planning stages of the wedding. They haven't picked a date yet. Once they do, it will mean that we have a wedding to go to. Anyway, I did some cleaning after I got home this afternoon and, well, I think that we will go to a movie tonight. How does that sound?" Matt opens the wine and puts some of it into the sauce.

"That sounds like a good idea. At least we are still dating." Tammy smiles as she hugs him.

"That's funny; do you think that our lives would change if we were married? The only difference would be that our names would be the same." Matt tastes the sauce with a spoon. "A little salt and pepper and, presto, it will be done."

"Who said that I would change my last name?" Tammy looks at Matt.

"I think that it would be best if you did because it would be a kind gesture toward the family and for the sake of our kids." Matt turns the sauce onto low heat to simmer.

"I'll have to think about that." Tammy leaves the kitchen for the bedroom to changing out of her work clothes.

By the time Matt has supper done and onto the plates, Tammy is already sitting and ready to eat. Matt brings the bottle of wine to the table and then the food. They eat in a quiet peace, something that has not happened in a long time for them. After supper, they do the dishes and then they get ready to go out to the theatre.

After the movie, Tammy and Matt walk the short distance back to the condo under a star-filled sky. At the condo, Matt lights up a smoke, walks up the stairs, and makes his way to the balcony that's just off of the living room.

When ten o'clock comes to pass, Matt makes his way to the living room to watch the news, as Tammy gets ready for bed. "Are you going to watch the news with me or are you going to bed right away?" Matt flicks on the local news.

"No, I think that I'm going to read a bit and then get some shut eye," Tammy says from the bedroom.

After the news is over, Matt picks up his book and turns on the lamp on the end table beside his chair. He continues to read from where he finished earlier.

It is six in the morning when Tammy's alarm is bleating. Reaching over to the clock to shut it off, she rolls out of bed and sees the empty space where Matt normally sleeps. Thinking nothing of it, she picks out her clothes for work and heads to the bathroom to get ready. This is the day she's been waiting on for the last week. It is Charles's return and she wants to be ready for it. But she is nervous. What does he want? What is he going to do? Why is he coming back? All the questions from days before run through her head as she showers. Getting out, she dries off, puts on her clothes and finishes getting ready for work.

Coming out of the bathroom, Tammy can see Matt sleeping in his chair. She makes her way into the kitchen to make her breakfast and coffee. As the coffee begins to brew, she pulls a bowl out of the cupboard and gets the cereal from the counter. She fills the bowl and sets the box back in place. Opening the fridge, she gets the milk and pours it over the cereal. After placing the milk back in the fridge, she gets a spoon and, by this time, the coffee is ready. She pours a cup and heads over to the table to enjoy her breakfast.

After finishing, Tammy puts her dishes to the sink. She looks at the time to see that it is 6:20. "Wake up, Matt," she says softly as she walks into the living room. "Matt, it's time to get up."

"What? Five more minutes," Matt responds in a sleepy voice.

"It's twenty after six. Coffee is made and I'm leaving for work." Tammy moves Matt's head to face her.

"Coffee...What...Work...OK." Matt rolls his head out of Tammy's hands.

Tammy smiles some as she watches Matt drift back to sleep. Then she goes to the closet, gets her coat, and walks down the stairs to put her shoes on. She shuts the door slowly and locks it. When she reaches the News, she notices that Rob isn't there. She gets the paper and leaves without saying a word.

As Tammy turns the corner, she sees an ambulance and cop cars sitting in front of her building. She rushes up to the one police-man and asks, "What's happening?"

"Just cleaning up the mess made from a suicide." The officer directs his attention back to the front doors of the building. About thirty minutes pass before all the officers and medical attendants leave the building's front steps with the body of a man.

Tammy looks at her watch to see that it is just after seven. She walks into the building and makes her way to the elevators. As she gets to her office door, she can't help but feel sorry for the family of the suicide victim. She walks in, hangs up her coat, sits down in her chair, and starts reading the paper.

When eight o'clock strikes, Carolin walks in the door of the office. Placing her coat on the coat rack, she walks into Tammy's office and sits down. "Good morning Tammy. The walk to the bus stop was cool this morning."

"It is the big day today. Charles is back and he will be here in less than fifty-five minutes. I don't know if I'm ready for him to come back. He left such an impression that he didn't want to be here last time." Tammy makes eye contact and puts the paper down on the desk.

"As I think I've said before; he might have changed in the last three years." Carolin leans toward the desk and picks up the paper. "You don't mind?"

"No, go ahead." Tammy gets up out of her chair. "I'll go and get his file."

The time goes by fast, and before they know it, the door of the office opens and Charles walks in. "Hard at work, I see. Are both of you going to be seeing me or what?" Charles enters Tammy's office and sits down in the chair next to Carolin.

"No, I was just leaving." Carolin gets up from the chair. "Have a good session, Tammy."

"I will. Charles, how are you today?" Tammy asks as Carolin closes the door behind her.

"I'm well. It's been three years since we parted ways." Charles takes off his hat. "So, how have you been?"

"I've been well. It's nice to see you again. I thought that after our last session you wouldn't be back." Tammy opens up his file and picks up a pen. "Is your boss sending you this time or are you here on your own free will?"

"This time it's for my reasons." Charles looks out the window. "Still the same view. Tammy, the first time I was here I didn't treat you with the respect that you deserved and I couldn't understand why you allowed me to do that to you. So this time, it's going to be different."

"I saw something in you and I wanted to help you, that is why. So how do you want to start today?"

"I've been thinking about that for the last few days. I think that I'll start by saying that I've been diagnosed with schizophrenia. I was just released from the hospital last Monday. I was in there for two months." Charles relaxes into the chair.

"Do you want to talk about it?"

"I do. This is for all the people that said that I should spend time in a mental institution. It's not a nice place because the people there are suffering from all types of mental illness. It's a very sad place to visit and it's an even worse place if you are one of the patients." Charles covers his eyes with his hand. "I woke up there and I didn't know how I got there. I remember my mother and aunt being there for the first week to visit me; other family members came to visit, as well. Then my mother left and my aunt would visit me when she had time."

"What did you do with your time when aunt wasn't there?"

"I did what I could do to keep myself from going crazy. Most of the time, I was writing out my life in a journal, and at other times, I drew. I would also play the piano for about an hour after each meal." Charles wipes a tear from his eye. "There must be a draft in here."

"It's OK, Charles. No one will know." Tammy hands him a tissue.

"My whole life was turned upside down. It was like I was in jail. I was on one of the locked wards. It took about three weeks until I was allowed off the ward for fifteen minutes, three times a day. I was only able to stay on the grounds of the hospital during that time." Charles wipes another tear with the tissue. "It was a week later that I was able to leave the hospital under the supervision of someone that they could trust—and only for two hours a day."

"Charles, how did you cope with those first three weeks? Not being allowed to leave the ward, I mean?"

"It was hard. When my aunt would visit, she would always bring me coffee and cookies from the coffee shop that we always went to on Spring Garden Road, which is a five-minute walk from the hospital. Those three weeks I don't think I was in any condition to leave the ward anyway. My body was getting used to the drugs. When I did get my passes, I would go down to one of the coffee shops on the main floor in the morning and sit there for ten minutes. For just that moment I'd feel normal then the walk back to the ward made me realize that that I wasn't. I would also sit in the chapel after supper and ask God for forgiveness and to walk with me on this new path that I found myself on."

"So you are on medication then. How do you feel about that?"

"I feel that I'm over medicated because I'm as high as I was when I smoked weed and it's the same high. It's sad to say, but your father said that I might not be able to return to work because of the medication I'm on and the fact that the hallucinations are not being controlled by the drugs."

"What will you do then?" Tammy puts down her pen.

"I'm moving back to Sova to be with my parents. They said that I could stay down here at my aunt's until I'm ready to travel." Charles clears his throat.

"So, what do you think about the illness that you are suffering? I mean, how do you feel about it?"

"It explains a lot about me. Ever since I was young, I knew there was something wrong with me. Now I have the answer and I'm able to move on with my life. It means that I will be on pills for the rest of my life, but I will be able to at least function and I'll educate myself about the illness so I can live a somewhat normal life." Charles turns to face Tammy. "There was one night when I was writing in my room when my nurse came in to check on me. She asked me what I was working on and I told her. She handed me my night pills and a glass of water. After that, she said something that made me think. She said, 'To suffer from a mental illness, you have to be an extremely intelligent person.' The thing that came to me was that you are a borderline genius, borderline insane, and it makes sense."

"It does. You said that it could be some time before you return to the workforce. What will you do with your time until then?"

"I'll get assistance from the government which will cover my medication and some of my bills. With the time I'll have, I think I'll work on my creative side and write a book about mental illness. I hope that it will help the world to see the problem that we have with the illnesses. You know, the pushing it into a dark room with the hope that it will go away."

"That sounds interesting. Do you know how you will write it?"

"I have a couple of ideas going around in my head. I think I'll have one of my characters be loosely based on my own life. It's just a thought right now. If I do it, it will most likely take me a few years." Charles turns back to the window.

"So that means that I'll be in it as a small role. What will you name it?" Tammy takes a sip of her water.

"I don't know yet, but I know how I'm going to start it. The first chapter is going to be in first person from the main character as he introduces the book. At the end of the chapter, he will say, 'Here is the story of my life.' It will be about everything that happened in my life and some stories that friends have told me over the years. What I'll be doing is writing about what I know," Charles chuckles.

"That sounds like a bestseller to me, and writing about what you know is something that makes the characters more real. That's positive thinking, Charles, and it's good to see that you're not giving up on life even though you have a mental illness. Most people who are diagnosed give up, but there are some like you who are born fighters and don't quit." Tammy picks up the pen and makes a note.

"Yeah, my parents didn't raise a quitter. You know? I do look up to them." Charles turns back to Tammy and continues. "They would call me on Sunday nights to see how I was doing when I was hospitalized. I'm glad they did that, even though I was mad at Mom for some reason that I can't really recall."

"When you are ready to move back to Sova, are your parents going to come down to pick you up or are you going to fly?"

"I don't know yet."

"Did you make any friends when you were in the hospital?" Tammy asks and Charles nods his head.

"I did, but they suffer from depression. You know, I don't remember being taken to the hospital by the police, I don't remember from December 25 till January 26 when I was woken up by your father. That's a whole month that I don't remember. My mom found me in my closet hiding without anything on."

"Maybe it's a good thing that you don't remember it. The human mind will protect itself in an array of different ways and that's one of them." Tammy looks at the clock and sees that it is almost ten o'clock. "Charles, that's all the time we have for today. Come back tomorrow at five and we'll continue. We will have more time at the end of the day."

"OK, I'll be here then. Thank you for allowing me to come back." Charles gets up from the chair and walks out of the office.

Tammy closes Charles's file and walks out to Carolin who's in the middle of a game of solitaire. "Not to stop you from what you are doing, but here's Charles's file." Tammy sets the file on Carolin's desk.

"I only started playing five minutes ago." Carolin looks up at Tammy. "Your ten o'clock is waiting and here is her file."

"Thanks." Tammy picks up the file. "Shannon Taylor, come on in." Tammy walks into her office as the young lady follows her. The rest of the morning goes like clockwork until lunch.

Coming out of her office, Tammy sets the file of the last person on Carolin's desk. "Are you ready for lunch, Tammy?" Carolin asks, picking up the file from the desk.

"I am. Let's change it up a little. Why don't we go to My Father's Mustache?" Tammy asks as Carolin puts the file away. "They are only across the street."

"Yeah, sounds good. Let's go."

Tammy and Carolin walked across Spring Garden Road to the restaurant. As they enter, they see that it isn't busy for lunch. They find a table by the window and wait for a server.

"So, how did the session go with Charles?" Carolin asks as she sets her hands on the table.

"It went well and I think that he apologized to me for the treatment that he put me through three years ago." Tammy taps her fingers on the table. "What's taking them?"

"I was just going to say that myself."

A few more minutes went by and no server so Tammy and Carolin get up to leave when a server walks over to them, "What can I get for you?"

"For one thing, service. We're leaving, so have a good day," Tammy says, and she and Carolin walk out the door. Walking back to the building they go into the café in their building.

"Ladies, what held you up today?" Michael walks up to their table.

"We thought to try something different and, well, My Father's Mustache didn't give us service until we were leaving," Tammy says, as she takes a menu from him.

"Well, then, would you ladies like to order and I'll get the chef to make your meal up right away?" Michael flips out his notepad.

"I think that I'll have the scallops this time," Tammy smiles, without even looking at the menu.

"Well, make it two orders," Carolin says.

"Not a problem, ladies, I'll get our new girl to get you two some water and coffee." Michael walks away from the table.

"So, what else can you say about Charles?"

"Well, not much really, but he is coming back tomorrow at five. If you want or if he will let you, you should sit in on the next session. We'll do it together and then you'll have an idea of who he is. What do you say?" Tammy asks as the new server sets the drinks on the table.

"Sure, if he will go for it."

Tammy and Carolin talk until their order arrives. They eat quickly and then head back to work.

The afternoon moves by swiftly and, before they know it, it's time to go home. Tammy walks out of the office and sets the last patient's file on Carolin's desk. "I'll see you in the morning, Carolin."

On Tammy's return home, she walks into the kitchen to see Matt only dressed from the waist down. He smiles at her as she shakes her head before heading to the bedroom to get changed. "Have you been like that all day?" Tammy yells from the bedroom.

"For most of it, why? As well, you don't need to yell." Matt turns the steaks that he's cooking for supper.

"Just wondering. I'm going to be working late for the next few days." Tammy walks back to the kitchen.

"Why is that?"

"I told one of my clients to come at five so that we wouldn't be rushed for time." Tammy gives Matt a hug.

"How nice, you're making time after you are normally off. What time should I be expecting you home at so I can have supper ready?" Matt moves Tammy out of the way and opens the oven to get the baked potatoes out.

"Six or six-thirty; I hope that it won't be a problem," Tammy says, as she picks the smaller of the two potatoes and places it on a plate. "So, what did you do today?"

"Nothing much. Read a book, that's about all. How was work for you?" Matt puts a steak on Tammy's plate.

"It was work and it went well," Tammy says, as she walks over to the table and sits down.

Matt sits down across from Tammy. They talk about the day as they eat. After supper, they do the dishes, and watch the news. When the news is over, Matt gets dressed and they go out for a walk along the waterfront as the sun sets over the city. "I hear that on the prairies the sunsets go forever. In the east, it is dark and in the west, the colours of the sunset linger on for hours." Matt pulls Tammy close as they watch the sky. "I guess it would be like a sunrise on the ocean here. I've never been out west, so I can't compare them."

"Maybe we could take a trip out west one day to see," Tammy says, as they sit down on a bench.

"We could, but it would mean that you would have to take some time off." Matt puts his arm around Tammy.

"I think that won't be a problem. Carolin and I are getting a person to do her job so she can do some counselling. It will mean that we can take time off and be able to cover for each other." Tammy leans her head on his shoulder.

"When is that happening?"

"We will be getting her next week from the school on a work term, and then we will be asking her to stay on for full time if she works out." Tammy looks up into Matt's blue eyes.

"That's good; I think we should get a coffee and head home."

They head to the Tim's Coffee House that is just down from the condo. As they walk in, Tammy notices Charles sitting with some men wearing suits. Charles, himself, is wearing one, as well. Tammy turns and walks behind Matt to the counter with the hope that Charles doesn't see her, but it is too late. Charles gets up and walks over to Tammy. "Funny to see you here. Are you alone?"

"No." Tammy pulls on Matt's coat. "This is my boyfriend, Matt."

Matt turns. "You are who?"

"Matt, this is one of my patients, Charles." Charles puts out his hand.

"Nice to meet you, Charles." Matt takes Charles's hand with a strong shake. "What do you do for a living?"

"I'm a chef-slash-businessman, but that doesn't matter. Tammy, I'll see you tomorrow. Nice to meet you, Matt." Charles turns and walks back to his table.

"Tammy, I know what kind of business he is in and it's not legal," Matt whispers in Tammy's ear.

"Matt, don't jump the gun. He probably has a reason to be in a suit. He might be meeting those men here for a coffee," Tammy whispers back. "You're next to order."

Matt walks up to the counter and orders two extra-large coffees.

"That will be four dollars," the cashier says, and another worker pours the coffee.

Matt pulls out the money and places it on the counter. "Thanks." Matt hands Tammy a cup. "Let's go." Tammy follows Matt out of the coffee shop. As they walk up the street to the condo, an expensive car drives by with Charles in the back seat and the men he was with in the front. Matt notices the car, but says nothing to Tammy.

Tammy and Matt reach the condo a few minutes later and Matt heads to the living room and sits in his chair. He picks up his book and starts to read.

"Matt, I think that we should do that more often," Tammy says, as she sits in her chair in the living room.

"Do what?" Matt lowers the book.

"Going for walks and that."

"We can do that for the rest of my holidays, but when I go back to work, I'll be getting home late." Matt lifts the book back up.

"Maybe if you are off early enough—like, let's say seven or eight—we could go for a walk then."

"Or we could go for walks when I have days off. That would make more sense because you know that I normally get home between nine and ten." Matt picks up his coffee and takes a sip.

"Do you mind if I turn the TV on?" Tammy picks up the remote.

"No, go ahead." Matt puts his coffee down on the end table.

As the hours pass, Tammy finishes watching the ten o'clock news and heads for bed. Matt continues to read the rest of his book and then falls asleep in his chair.

CHAPTER twelve

Thursday morning comes quickly and Tammy's alarm goes off. She rolls to the side that Matt normally sleeps on and sees that he isn't there. Getting out of bed, she puts on her housecoat and walks out of the bedroom to the kitchen to make coffee. Walking into the living room, she wakes Matt up from his sleep. "Matt, time to get up." She pinches his nose.

"Wha..." Matt's sleepy voice says as he opens his eyes.

"The coffee is being made, and I'm going to get ready for work." Tammy walks to the bathroom. About twenty minutes later, she heads for the bedroom to get dressed.

Matt makes his way from his chair in the living room to the kitchen to make himself a cup of coffee. He then goes back to his chair and picks up the remote and turns the TV on. He surfs the channels and finds the Morning Metro News. "Tammy, they are saying that it might rain today. If it is, give me a call when you're done work, and I'll pick you up."

"I'll do that. Don't forget that I'm working late tonight." Tammy comes out of the bedroom and gets a coffee ready in her travel mug. "Matt, why did you sleep in your chair last night?"

"I tried to get comfortable in bed, but couldn't, so I came back to my chair and read until about one before dozing off." Matt takes a sip of his coffee.

"I see. Well, I'll see you tonight and I'll call when I'm finished work." Tammy walks down the stairs to the door and puts on her shoes and coat. "See you later."

Tammy walks up to The News for her daily paper. "Good morning, Rob."

"Good morning, Tammy. How are you today?" Rob smiles.

"I'm well, and it is a good day to be alive." Tammy sets the paper down.

"Just the paper today?"

"Here's the money and a smile to go with it." Tammy puts the $1.25 on the counter.

"Tammy, have a wonderful day, and when the next Mental Health Weekly is in, I'll hold one for you."

Tammy smiles, walks out the doors, and heads to work. As she gets to work, she sees a raincloud in the distance. *Another rainy day on the east coast*, she thinks as she walks in the doors of the building. This time, it seemed different for her. The day had started with a strange feeling; it was almost sad. The wind was raw and moist and there was an odd sound to it as it whistled through the trees along the streets. And there was something else that she couldn't put her finger on.

The last time she felt this way a hurricane had struck the area two years before called hurricane Juan. That year had its hardships for Tammy. Her grandmother had passed away, four of her clients had killed themselves, and that summer, Matt was working down at Pier Twenty-Two where the hours were long.

The eerie feeling put Tammy into a state of confusion and, when she gets to her office, she opens the door quickly and looks behind as if someone was there. Seeing no one, she enters and hangs her coat up. She sits down and sees there's a message on her phone. *Maybe this is the reason for this feeling that I'm having*, she thinks.

The message is from one of her clients to say that he would be missing his appointment for that day. *That can't be it*, she thinks as she opens the paper.

It's 8:30 when Carolin shows up for work. Putting her coat on the coat rack, she walks into Tammy's office "How are you doing today, Tammy?"

"I have this eerie feeling that something is going to happen today. Other than that, I'm fine." Tammy folds the paper and sets it down on the desk.

"I got that feeling, too. I think that this storm is going to be big." Carolin picks up the paper.

"It's not that—or is that a metaphor for Charles?" Tammy makes eye contact.

"You said it, not me. I think that having him come in after hours is not the smartest thing." Carolin shakes her head. "Just to let you know, I'll be here in the office until he leaves."

"I don't think that anything will happen. I think that the feeling is much bigger than that," Tammy says, as Carolin opens up the paper. Tammy looks at the front page for a second time. "There it is!"

"There's what?" Carolin puts the paper down.

"Fifty-five people found dead in a mass grave in Prussia. I saw Charles last night with two men in suits. I remember three years ago that Charles said that he was part of an organization that is in all types of things, and not just drugs. That makes sense now; Charles had to leave the west because of that. Can you pass me the paper?" Tammy puts out her hand. "They say that they figure that the grave was dug some three to five years ago. That's got to be it."

"Whatever drugs that you are on, I want some. I don't think that Charles would kill someone. With that being said, we have to get to get ready and help people." Carolin stands up and, taking the paper from Tammy, walks out the door and closes it.

The morning sessions come and go as usual for Tammy. By the time lunch comes, the eerie feeling is gone. Carolin goes into her office as the last of the morning clients leaves. "Time for lunch, Carolin?" Tammy asks as she stands up from her chair. She turns to look out the window to see that the rain is coming down hard. "Some days I wonder why I stay living down here."

"It's not that bad. We had a good winter and, well, so far, a good spring. Are you ready to go for lunch?"

"Yeah, let's go." Tammy moves around her desk.

Tammy and Carolin make their way to the restaurant on the main floor. They sit down at one of the tables by the window that looks out to the Public Gardens. This time, a different waiter comes to their table. "What can I get for you ladies?" he asks as he puts the menus down in front of them.

"I'll have a coffee and a BLT with salad, maple balsamic dressing." Tammy hands him the menu.

"A glass of water and the goat cheese salad." Carolin hands him the menu. "Where is Michael?"

"I don't see him; maybe he has to take the day off. Carolin, sorry about this morning. I was just feeling strange."

"Don't worry about it. We all get those days. It's in the past and that is where it will stay. So what did you do last night?" Carolin asks as the waiter sets her water and Tammy's coffee down on the table.

"Matt and I went for a walk along the boardwalk and then got coffee. I saw Charles in the coffee shop and he came up to me to say hi." Tammy takes a sip of her coffee.

"He did. Well, that's a good thing, I guess."

"I think that is why I had this eerie feeling today. He was dressed in a full suit and he was with two other men in suits. As well, I think he is into something that he never really got out of when he left Cunnings."

"Crime, drugs, what? From what I remember of him when he came to us the first time, he was always in jeans and a tee shirt with black polished army boots. So a suit...maybe he was doing some modeling and that was part of the get-up—you never know." Carolin picks up her water and takes a drink.

"Well, what would be the need for the other two?"

"You really need a holiday, and when we get our new assistant, you should take two weeks to get away. You deserve it: three years, it's time for one."

As Tammy and Carolin eat, a silence falls between them. The lunch hour passes and, before they know it, it's time to return to work. The afternoon passes with four other people opening up to Tammy who, with a listening ear, gives them advice on their problems. Five o'clock approaches and Charles is in the waiting room. Tammy opens the door and lets her four o'clock out. "Have a good day, Kim. I'll see you next week." Tammy turns to Charles and says, "Are you ready, Charles?"

"I am. I guess I'll talk to you later, Carolin." Charles gets up from the chair and walks through the open door of Tammy's office.

"Charles, do you mind if Carolin sits in on our session?" Tammy asks as Charles walks past her.

"I think that would be a problem because she has never sat in on any of our sessions. It would take too long for her to get up to speed on me. You know what I mean?" Charles sits down in the chair in front of Tammy's desk.

"Sorry, Carolin." Tammy looks at Carolin.

"It's no problem; I'll be here until you are done tonight." Carolin turns back to her computer.

Closing the door, Tammy says, "So, we meet again."

"We do. I hope that you didn't take me the wrong way last night. I just wanted you to see me in a suit because here all you see me in is jeans and tee shirts. Where were we yesterday? I think that we were talking about the hospital. Those two months is how the last three years ended and, for the most part, this is how my chapter in Metro is going to end." Charles looks down at the front of the desk.

"What do you mean by your chapter in Metro ending?" Tammy opens up the file.

"I'm starting from square one when I move back to Sova. I'm not staying here. I have no job, no place to live other than at my aunt's, so I'm moving home." Charles turns his head to the window.

"When are you leaving?" Tammy picks up a pen.

"Not sure. I think that we talked about that yesterday. I'll tell you about the last three years." Charles takes a breath. "After our last session, I went down to Mark's for a coffee. It was slow at that time there so I had my selection of seats. I sat next to the windows overlooking the harbour. I turned my head toward the door each time it opened to see who was coming in. The last time I looked, it was Sir and he saw me. He got his coffee, came over to my table, and sat down."

"It must have been nice to have a coffee with him."

"It wasn't. It brought back the memories of what I did in Cunnings. I wished that it was a chance meeting, but I knew it wasn't. He knew that I'd be there. He said to me when I was leaving Cunnings that I'd always be a Ghost. He told me that there was a meeting down here in Metro and that I was expected to attend it with him. My role as a drug runner was over, and now there was a different role for me. I told him that I was through with being a Ghost." Charles runs his hand through his hair.

"How did he take that?"

"Not good. He reminded me of the favour he gave me to get out of the criminal world by letting me leave Cunnings alive. The meeting was a couple of days later in one of the hotels downtown here. I walked into the hotel with ripped jeans, black army boots, and a white tee shirt, much like I am today. Talk about a good first impression to a room with ten men with suits on, not including Sir. The meeting lasted about two hours. I was told what my new job was, where my office was, where to eat, where to drink, how to dress, and everything else you could imagine." Charles looks back to Tammy.

"So what you are telling me is that you went back to work for them." Tammy makes eye contact.

"I told them no. The only downfall is that they thought I needed some time to think about it. So they said that we would have another meeting a week later where Sir wouldn't be present. I walked out of the banquet room and the hotel with Sir following me. I got to the light and Sir put his hand on my back and said that it was a good offer and that I would be able to use my schooling for something. I told him that my life didn't need a helping hand and I could find a job doing something, even if it was cooking again. He told me I was still like a son to him and that he wanted me to think about the offer. As well, he wanted to have lunch with me so that we could talk about things." Charles breaks eye contact and looks back out the window.

"What kind of things did he want to talk to you about?"

"Sir was like a father to me when I lived in Cunnings. He was more of a father than my own was. He cared for me, unlike my dad who was always drunk and mad at the world. For those four years he helped me, and even now he was the first person I called when I was in the hospital. The lunch that we had that day was at Bish, down on the waterfront. Sir told me that he was just looking out for me and that he felt I could use a hand from the Ghosts. I told him I saw what he was trying to do, but that I didn't want the hand. He said to me that he had gotten a call from down here that I was mixed up with the wrong people. I didn't see Charles Mayfield and Matt Bennett as bad people, but now I only wish death to them both. I'm not one to make judgment on other races, but for the blacks, I'll never trust them again. Sir left the next day and told me to take the job. I went to the next meeting and told them that I would start, but on my terms." Charles leans back into the chair.

"Charles, you make a bold statement there with the blacks. What did Charles Mayfield and Matt Bennett do to you?" Tammy sets the pen down.

"Them two idiots, I'll tell you. Charles took advantage of my kindness. He told me a story about a tough life and that all he wanted to do was to be an actor. He asked me for money—or I should say threatened me that if I didn't give him money, he would have his people rob me. I gave him $2,500 in total. I should have seen him for what he was, but I was blind. I will give you the short version of the Matt Bennett story: robbed me twice. I just wanted friends and, well, I never made any down here. It wasn't just them two, Tim Ward, and his band of gay friends. He was white so it is not just the blacks. Over the last three years, people have taken advantage of me because I left what I did in Cunnings in the past and I wanted to start a new life with real people. All I got was idiots." Charles shakes his head.

"I guess you have had a tough road down here, too. Prussia and here. I'd say Cunnings, but you were in a different world there."

"Yeah, in Cunnings I had money, drugs, girls, and anything that I wanted. I tried, Tammy. Anyway, when I took my job with the Ghosts down here, I was in charge of the business end of things. Who did what, what went where, and so on. I was the under-boss for the area. Nothing happened without my knowing about it, everything from new restaurant openings to drug traffic. By the time I started, my problems ended because I had become a big fish in a small pond. I didn't need friends anymore. I still stayed in contact with Jen, but that was it. I soon became like I was in Cunnings all over again, but this time I was the one behind the picture who couldn't be caught. About a year went by before I saw Sir again. He flew down and we went for a meal at Bish. He said that he had been keeping a tab on me and that he liked what was being said about me. I wasn't happy, though. I was into doing drugs again, not just weed. I was trying to escape from life. I was alone, even though I have family in the area. I started to drink again and wished for death. So in the reality of it, it was just like Cunnings but I wasn't running drugs." Charles covers his eyes.

"Everyone has their demons, Charles, and one of those is to use drugs and alcohol. How long have you been clean for, or are you still using?"

"Well, I guess it has been three or four months now. My life is a mess and I am just starting to pick up the pieces. That's why I'm moving back home. When I called Sir from the hospital, he told me he would come and see me. A week went by before he showed up. He came onto the ward and walked to my room. Just seeing his face was enough to give me hope. He asked my doctor if he could take me off the ward to a restaurant. Your dad said yes. Sir and I walked out of the hospital to a waiting car. When I got into the backseat with Sir, I broke down. Sir said that it was OK to cry. He held me as the driver pulled away from the hospital and down the street toward the waterfront. He was there for me, Tammy. He said that he would put the paperwork through to have me labelled inactive for the Ghosts. I'd still be a Ghost, but I would be able to go back to active when I wanted. As of now, I'm inactive. The men you saw me with yesterday, one is my driver and the other is a bodyguard. They will be with me until I leave Metro." Charles tries to stop himself from crying.

"No one is going to know if you cry. You're safe here," Tammy hands him a tissue. "Charles, why have you come back to see me after three years? I want to know the truth."

"The truth is that I never stopped thinking about you. You were nice to me and I should have never stopped coming. I could have gotten through the last three years a lot better. I think that if I had stayed, I never would have gone back to drugs and booze. That is in the past now and I have to live with it." Charles wipes a tear with the tissue.

"You can let it go and take the lessons that you have learned in the last three years as life experience." Tammy closes the file.

"God, you think He has been there to save me? What good has He been to me? I was dealt a bad hand and I have been playing it the best I can. You say lessons—all I know is hate and that is how it has been for years. The odd time it plays in my favour, but I'm always on the outside looking in. The decisions that I have made, God didn't make. I did. It was me who became a Ghost up in Cunnings. It was me who thought that Charles Mayfield and Matt Bennett were trustworthy and I was wrong. God hasn't been there for me. Maybe it was God who sent my mother to find me hiding naked in my closet, I don't know. Let's just say that I have lost faith in a higher power." Charles makes eye contact with Tammy. "I see that the file is closed. Does that mean that the session is over?"

"No, I think that I'll just listen to you, Charles. The fact that you have lost faith in a higher power is just showing that God is waiting for you to accept Him. Charles, the pain that is on your face is the same pain that I saw three years ago. It's time that you let go of that pain and start to live your life."

"Pain, that's what I have always known next to hate. How do you let go of that? How do you live after your innocence has been taken from you at a young age? How do you trust when it has been ripped from you? I tried to start over and it didn't work. I'm trying it again back home in Sova. Maybe there, I will find what I truly need or it will be a bullet. I've seen the faces of all men and it sickens me. Maybe I'll find something out there that I haven't seen before." Charles looks back outside.

"If you let go of the pain, your outlook on things will change."

"Sure, I think that I'll see you tomorrow and we'll try to figure this pain thing out." Charles gets to his feet. "Have a good night, Tammy." Charles leaves the office.

A few minutes later, Tammy walks out of her office. "Carolin, are you ready to go?"

"I am. I think that I will be calling a cab because it's raining." Carolin starts picking up the phone.

"Matt and I can give you a ride; he's coming to get me."

"OK." Carolin puts down the phone.

Tammy and Carolin get their coats and leave the office for the elevator. At the main level, they see Charles getting into a car. He turns back, waves, and closes the door. As the car leaves, Matt pulls up. The ladies make their way outside and into the car. "Matt, you don't mind if we drop Carolin off at her place?"

"No, it's raining so an extra trip is no problem. How was your day, Tammy?" Matt puts the car into gear and pulls onto the street.

"It was all right. And yours?" Tammy looks out the side window.

"Well, I got a call from Chef today asking me how my time off was going. Other than that I spent the most of the day reading. How was your day Carolin?"

"It was a day, nothing to write home to mom about."

As they drive through the city, the rain starts to become heavier. The traffic is light for a rush hour that seems to be moving slow. Matt makes his way through the streets taking the short cuts to Carolin's place. When he pulls up to Carolin's, he puts the car into park. "Well, here you are, Carolin. That will be five dollars," Matt laughs.

"See you in the morning Tammy. Thanks for the ride Matt, see you later," Carolin gets out of the car.

"Let's go home, Matt," Tammy looks over to Matt.

Matt pulls away from Carolin's and starts on the way back to the condo. "Tammy, I had a thought today and it was about you and me. For the last three years that we have been together, we have grown into a strong couple. I think that the thing that makes us strong is that our time together is quality time. I know that we have our fights but what relationship doesn't? I found that I truly love you and I just want you to know that. I know that sometimes it's hard for me to show it but I do," Matt pulls up to a stop at a light.

"Thanks Matt. I love you as well. What are we having for supper tonight?"

"I was thinking that we would go to Opa for something different. So what do you think?"

"We can do that, it's been a while since we were to a restaurant and had someone take care of us. I can't remember how long it has been since we went there last," Tammy places her hand on his leg.

"The last time was your birthday. I remember that because I had asked for the day off from work. The time before that was when my parents were down for a visit."

"I remember that visit because they asked us when they would be seeing grandchildren or a wedding," Tammy rubs Matt's leg.

"Yeah. That meant that they approved of you. They always ask about you when I'm talking to them. Well here is the restaurant, are you ready to eat?" Matt asks as he parks the car.

Tammy says yes and they get out of the car. They run across the street and into Opa. As they enter, Matt walks up to the stairs with Tammy following him. A waiter shows them to their table and gives them menus. The table is beside one of the windows looking out onto the street, and with Matt's view he can see Pizza Corner. The night is young and Tammy can't figure out why Matt has asked her out to the restaurant for supper. That's when she has a thought, either he is going to pop the question or there is something else.

The waiter returns to their table with water and takes their orders. Matt orders the lamb and Tammy orders the sea bass. The waiter leaves the table and that is when it happens. Matt pulls out a box from his coat pocket. "Tammy," he opens the box, "will you be mine forever?"

"I will," Tammy says with a smile on her face and tears of joy started to run down her face.

"I've been holding onto this ring for the last month. I just needed to find the right day to ask you and then I made the reservations here yesterday. I wanted to do this so many different ways and I couldn't for the life of me think of anything special. Your mom and I picked out the ring. I mean she helped me pick it out. I had to also think of a way that you wouldn't see the bill, so I used my personal credit card. I love you Tammy and after the last few nights I thought that it was time. We're not getting younger and well, I think that it's time that we both settle down with a positive direction of where we are going. I found out today that my direction is with you," Matt picks up Tammy's left hand and put the ring on her ring finger.

"I love you Matt," Tammy wipes the tear from her face. "Now my makeup is going to be a mess."

"It looks fine Tammy," then the waiter comes over to the table with a red rose.

"It looks like that you took out all the stops."

"Your food is almost ready," the waiter says with a smile and then leaves the table.

It is Friday morning and the alarm clock is going off. Reaching up, Matt turns it off. "Tammy, are you awake?" he asks, softly.

"I've been awake for the last twenty minutes. I just felt like staying in bed for a little longer. Will you go and make me some coffee?" Tammy rolls over to face Matt.

"Sure," Matt gets out of bed. As he walked to the kitchen to brew the coffee, Tammy makes her way to the bathroom to take a shower. Matt goes back to the bedroom to get dressed. Looking at the time on the clock, Matt sits down on the bed picking up Tammy's nightgown off the floor. A few minutes later, Tammy came into the bedroom with a towel wrapped around her. "I'll give you a ride to work this morning, that way you will have a few extra minutes to have coffee with me."

"Thanks Matt but the walk helps me wake up," Tammy starts to gets dressed for work.

"Well I guess if that is the case, I'll walk with you if that is OK." Matt gets up from the bed.

"That would be nice of you. What are your plans for today?"

"Not sure yet, I think that I'll go down to the farmers market and pick out something good for supper. Then I might take some time at Point Pleasant Park. You know, watch the ships come in and out of port. Want me to pour your coffee Tammy?" Matt heads to the kitchen to pour the coffees.

"Sure," Tammy makes her way out of the bedroom all ready for work. Matt hands her to-go mug to her. "Well, are we ready to go?"

"Let me get my jacket and we will be off," Matt walks to the closet to grab his coat. As Tammy is getting hers, Matt sits at the bottom of the stairs putting on his boots.

Tammy makes her way down the stairs and put on her shoes as Matt opens the door. Tammy gets back to her feet, walks out the door and down the cement stairs that lead to the sidewalk. Matt locks the door as he walks out onto the top stair and looks down at Tammy. "Let's go, Matt. What are you looking at, Matt?"

"You and thinking how lucky I am to have you as a girlfriend, fiancée, and future wife and mother of my children." Matt walks down the stairs.

"It's *our* children," Tammy says, and chuckles.

"I give you a compliment and you pick it apart," Matt grins.

Tammy and Matt walk up the street arm in arm like two lovebirds singing a song, almost like puppy love. When they get to The News, they walk in. Matt heads over to see if the new issue of Planet Chef was in as Tammy gets her normal. Tammy walks up to the till, "Good morning, Rob."

"Good morning, Tammy. The regular, or should I wait for Matt to come up to the till?" Rob rings in the paper.

"Matt," Tammy tries to get his attention.

"I'll be right there," Matt walks over to Tammy.

"Matt, did you find what you were looking for?" Rob asks, before Tammy pays for the paper.

"When does the next Planet Chef come in, Rob?"

"Not until Monday, so it's just the paper. Friday edition is $2.50." Rob rings the sale in. As Tammy goes to pay Rob, he sees the ring on her left hand. "Well, well, congratulations, Tammy. Tell me it's not him," he smiles, pointing to Matt.

"It is. Last night was the night," Tammy says, putting the paper under her arm.

"Well, Matt, you take care of her. And, Tammy, the wedding books are in that far corner. You two have a great day, and I'll probably see you both Monday," Rob says, and Tammy and Matt make their way out the door.

They walk up the street and make the turn that leads them to the office building. Arm in arm, they walk. Matt feels that his life would be complete if only this walk could last all morning, but he knows that Tammy has to work. As they reach the office building, Matt hugs Tammy and kisses her. "Have a good day at work, I'll see you when you get home." Matt kisses her one last time.

Tammy makes it through the glass doors and looks back to see Matt crossing the street and going into the Public Gardens. She turns and walks over to the elevators. After waiting only a minute, the elevator's doors open. She gets in and presses the button for her floor.

It was a different day, a new day. Tammy couldn't do anything but think how she is going to tell Carolin and her parents. She sees her relationship with Matt in a different light. It was like the end of a long trip that had its ups and downs.

As Tammy unlocks the door to the office, a picture of what she always wanted is revealed to her. She sees the perfect wedding with her family and Matt's, Carolin being right by her side. The dresses, suits, flowers, food, church, and pictures: she sees it all and it makes her happy.

Tammy closes the door behind her and hangs her coat up. Making her way to her office, she sits down and starts to read the paper. About an hour passes before Carolin shows up for work.

Carolin takes off her coat and hangs it beside Tammy's and then proceeds to Tammy's office. As she sits down, Carolin sees the ring. "You got to be kidding. He did it, didn't he?"

"Who did what?" Tammy puts the paper down.

"Matt, he really did it and you didn't call me."

"I thought that I would tell you today, but I guess you see the ring," Tammy smiles.

"You know what this means? Wedding plans and we're going to have fun. First, the date has to be decided on, then the dress. After the dress, it's the flower shop. No, no, no, the cake. Oh, this is going to be fun. Tammy, I'm so excited." Carolin claps her hands.

"I'd hate to see you if I was expecting," Tammy smiles.

"That will come soon enough. How did he ask you?" Carolin tries to hold back her emotions.

"Last night at Opa."

"Well, let me see the ring." Carolin gets closer to the desk. "I wonder how much it's worth. Do you think Matt would spend a paycheque or two on it?"

"I'm not too worried on how much he paid for it, but it is nice. He said that Mom was with him when he got it." Tammy looks at the ring.

"I'd think that he would have asked me, not your mom. He must have asked your dad for your hand first. He must have said yes, because you have the ring! So, when are you telling your parents?" Carolin takes the paper out of Tammy's hand.

"I think I will call them right now and then it will be time for us to do our jobs. Don't forget that Charles is here at five."

Carolin gets up as Tammy picks up the phone to call her parents and give them the news. She walks out of Tammy's office, walks over to her desk, and turns on her computer. She then walks over to the other office where all the files are kept to pull out the day's client files.

The morning goes by quickly, even though there are two new clients who have never been to a counsellor before. As the last of the morning's appointments ends, Tammy comes out of her office and goes over to the door. Looking back, she asks, "Are you ready for lunch?"

"Yeah, just give me a second to put these files away." Carolin gets up and walks to the other office. "Where are we going for lunch?"

"Well we could go to the Lord Nelson Hotel today, or we can go downstairs like normal."

"Let's try the hotel for a change." Carolin walks through the door.

Tammy locks the door as Carolin waits by the elevators. Tammy walks over to her with a half-smile on her face. "You know, Carolin, I've been waiting for this moment for the last year."

"What moment is that?"

"Well, Matt asking me to marry him. I thought there for a while that it wouldn't happen." Tammy follows Carolin to the elevator.

"He took his time to make sure that it was the right thing for him to do. It's a man thing, when they are sure, they are there at one hundred percent, and if they're not, they leave you hanging. That's one of the reasons I have stopped looking for a man; I'll let him find me."

When they arrive on the main floor of the building, the elevator doors open and Tammy and Carolin walk out. As they get to the glass doors of the building, they walk out and head to their right towards the Lord Nelson, which is just a few blocks away from their office.

Tammy and Carolin walk in silence to the hotel. When they get to the doors, they open them up to see the grand interior of the oldest hotel in Metro. They walk to the restaurant and wait to be seated.

"For two?" a waiter asks, walking up to Tammy.

"Yes, for the two of us," Tammy says, and then they follow the waiter to one of the tables by windows.

"What would you ladies like to drink?" the waiter asks as he set two menus down on the table.

"Coffee and a glass of water for me." Tammy sits down on one of the chairs across from Carolin.

"I'll have the same." Carolin picks up the menu.

"Our lunch special today is pan-fried white fish with a lemon dill cream sauce for twelve dollars," the waiter says, then leaves to get their drinks. On his return, he asks, "Are you ready to order?"

"I'll have the special." Tammy closes the menu and hands it to him.

"I think I'll have this sweet and sour pulled pork sandwich." Carolin hands the menu to the waiter, as well.

"Thank you, ladies. Both are very good choices." the waiter leaves to place the order with the kitchen.

"Tammy, are you going to get married in a church or in the banquet room of the hotel?"

"I don't know. Matt doesn't go to church and, well, neither do I. That's something that Matt and I will have to talk about." Tammy puts some sugar and cream in her coffee.

"Well, you are only going to get married once, so you should do it right," Carolin says, with excitement in her voice.

Tammy turns her head to look out the window. "I know that you are excited about this and, yes, you will be part of the planning but my attention is on this next session with Charles."

"You have always been about work, so I hope that it doesn't interfere with your wedding day. Tammy, there is more to life than work, and you of all people should know that. Take a minute and separate yourself from work and be human. Be like who you are when you are at home or when it's the weekend."

"I'm not all about work."

"When it's any time during the day between eight-thirty to five or later, you are different and, lately with Charles being back, you're taking it home with you. Face it, Tammy, how often does your work affect your relationship with Matt or your other friends, much less your parents? I'm simply trying to take your mind off work for a second to talk about this new development with Matt and you. This morning, you were OK with it, and now you are trying to push it aside like it is last week's news." Carolin takes a drink of her water.

"Carolin…" Tammy says.

"You know, life is about choices and it's up to us to make the right decision, whatever that is. Tammy, once we have our new assistant in the next week or so, you're taking some time off and I will take on your cases until you get back."

"Carolin, I'm fine. Thanks for your concern," Tammy says, as the food is set on the table.

"Ladies, is there anything else I can get for you?" the waiter asks.

"No, we're good," Carolin says, and the waiter walks away.

Tammy and Carolin eat their lunch and, when it comes time to pay, Carolin gets up and follows the waiter and pays. As Tammy and Carolin walk back to the office, Carolin asks, "Are you mad at me?"

"A little bit."

"I'm just being a friend and sometimes you need to hear the truth, whether you want to or not. That's life, and out of all your friends, we have known each other the longest. We grew up together and I know who you are. You need some time off to relax, and when you get back we will both be counselling," Carolin says, as they cross the street.

"Yeah." Tammy takes a deep breath.

When Tammy and Carolin arrive back at the office they go back to work. The afternoon appointments go well and it's closing in on five o'clock when Tammy is finishing up with her last patient.

When Tammy comes out of her office, Charles is sitting in the waiting room with a binder full of paper. Tammy hands Carolin the file on the last client. "Come on in, Charles."

Charles gets up out of the chair and follows Tammy into her office. As he gets to her desk, he sets down the binder and sits down. "So, how are we today?"

"I'm doing well, Charles. What's with the binder of paper?" Tammy sits down behind her desk.

"We will get to that later. Where were we yesterday?" Charles makes eye contact.

"We were going to start on how you can deal with the pain that you have inside. Where does it come from?" Tammy flips open his file.

"You know, or did you forget that? To remind you, it comes from Prussia and the abuse that I suffered there. The abuse I mean is my childhood and how I never got to be a child. I was alone for those years. Or wait a second, I did have a friend. One friend, Tammy. That's where it comes from." Charles turns towars the window.

"Well, that's a start. Did you ever return to Prussia after you moved away?"

"I did, but I messed up that trip. I was high on cocaine and caused damage to the relationship I had with one teacher. If I could say sorry to Miss Dillman, I would, but I don't think she would listen to me now." Charles closes his eyes.

"Have you tried to contact her?"

"I did and, well, it didn't go so well. That's fine with me. I went my way and, well, my life happens."

"What happens to you when the thoughts of Prussia come into your mind now?"

"I feel like going out and finding those people who tortured me and putting about five bullets into them, but that wouldn't stop the nightmares that I have almost every night. Every night when I go to sleep I think that I'm dreaming and, when I wake up, I will be back in Prussia. That is the torment that I live with, so you tell me, how do I get rid of this pain?" Charles opens his eyes.

"You can move on and only look forward from this point. Give them forgiveness and live for today."

"You know, Tammy, life has its ups and downs. God puts us into situations to see if we will get through them or not. That's the thing you need to know. And now I'll tell you about this binder." Charles gets up.

"This file you have on me is the lie that is my life and this binder is the truth of who I am. Goodbye, Tammy, I have already given forgiveness and moved on. Another day, another life." Charles walks out of the office.

Tammy picks up the binder, opens it to a page, and walks over to the window. After reading a couple of lines, she looks and sees

Charles getting into a waiting car. She looks back down at the binder and sees a folded note on the floor with her name on it that Charles left for her. The letter says:

> *Tammy, over the last three years, I have schooled myself,*
> *been a model, and followed my love for cooking. I have*
> *been on the outside looking in all my life and things are*
> *never going to change unless I change them. I have goals*
> *and dreams that I will make come true in my lifetime.*
> *I have had the hard road all my life and that is what*
> *gives me the strength to get through each and every day.*
> *When I first came to you, I was lost; not knowing which*
> *way was up. Over those first few weeks, I began to see*
> *the path again. Thank you for helping me find my way*
> *again. If you do decide to read the words on these pages,*
> *you will see me for who I truly am, but please don't judge*
> *me for the monster that I was.*
>
> *Charles*

Tammy walks back to her chair and sits down. About five minutes later, Carolin walks into the office. "Carolin, I think that is the last time we will see Charles Davis."

"Well, our lives will go on and so will his," Carolin says, closing the door and sitting down.